Enjoy!

C.C. Zantou

MW00711110

Iced at Midnight

Iced at Midnight

by
C. E. Zaniboni

Gypsy Shadow Publishing

Iced at Midnight
by
C. E. Zaniboni

Gypsy Shadow Publishing, LLC.
Lockhart, TX
www.gypsyshadow.com

Library of Congress Control Number: 2015938148

eBook ISBN: 978-1-61950-242-0
Print ISBN: 978-1-61950-255-0

Published in the United States of America

First eBook Edition: April 1, 2015
First Print Edition: April 10,2015

Dedication

I'd like to dedicate this book to my late dear friend, Bobbie McGrath, for her tireless effort in pushing me to finish and whose help I couldn't have done without. Love and miss you, Bobbie.

Chapter One

I looked up at the stars twinkling in a cold December sky and kicked at the dirty snow that a lumbering plow had just deposited in my path. *Thanks a lot, pal.* I shoved my hands into the pockets of my worn parka and exhaled. Right now, I should be enjoying the comfort of a warm bed and an even warmer female, instead of trudging down the winter streets of my hometown, Gammil's Point, Maine.

"Stop feeling sorry for yourself, Walleski," I muttered, pulling my watch cap down tight over my ears. I'd had another fight with my girl and she'd sent me packing. At least we don't live together. I couldn't seem to please her no matter what I did. Just the other night she'd flown into a tizzy when I'd smiled at a girl at the pizza place downtown. *It was just a smile, for heaven's sake. Dames.* I shook my head.

I drew abreast of the old Pike place and stopped. A snowman leered at me from the front yard of the abandoned property—minus a nose. He had all the other usual stuff, just no nose. Only an empty hole where one had been.

I frowned, looking around for the poor guy's honker. Shit. I really needed a cigarette. Too bad they were in the glove box of my car. I pulled out a stick of gum and unwrapped it. Poor substitute, but it would have to do. I folded it up and popped it in my mouth. I walked closer to get a better look at the snowman and gulped. There, partially hidden in a snowdrift was a man's body with something sticking out of his ear. A carrot. I almost swallowed my gum as I did a double take. *Shit!* My night had just gone from bad to worse. I yanked my cell from my pocket and dialed.

"Hey, Smitty, it's me, Walleski. I'm out at the Pike place looking at a snowman without his nose and the stiff whose ear is wearing it." I listened to his smart-assed reply. "No, his name isn't Frosty. Look, send a car. It's freezing out here."

I ended the call and eyed the dead guy. Young. Late twenties, early thirties. I stomped my feet to try to keep the circulation going. It was *damned* cold out. As a former cop turned private investigator, I'd seen a few bodies in my day, but none done in with a carrot. Pretty strange choice for a weapon, although I'd read about another case where a guy was killed with an icicle to the ear, so I knew it was possible.

Good thing I'd decided to take a walk to clear my head, otherwise the poor guy might have laid here for days. *Where the hell are the police?*

As if in answer to a prayer, a squad car glided to a stop in front of me. I hadn't realized I'd been walking in the middle of the road. The massive cop who got out looked like a tank with legs. Dexter Phillips. I'd tangled with him on more than one occasion, here and when we'd been in the Army together, stationed in 'Nam.

"Okay, Walleski, where's the body?" He stood like a statue in front of me, hand resting on his piece. I knew he had an itchy trigger finger.

I motioned for him to follow and led the way. I got the creeps looking at the frozen face of the snowman while a body lay not far away. Dexter bent down and felt of the corpse's neck. Did he think the guy had miraculously come back to life? What an asshole.

"Okay, he's beyond help."

No shit, I thought, wriggling my toes in the beat-up sneakers I'd foolishly worn. I watched him pull out his cell phone and punch in a number. He saw me looking at him and turned his back. *Dickhead.*

He turned to face me, a frown on his face. "The rest of the crew is on the way. Why don't we have a little chat, Walleski, starting with what you're doing out here in the middle of the night." Dexter waved me toward the unit. I started to get in the front seat. He shook his head and opened the rear door.

I got in. "Not good enough to grace you with my presence in the holy front seat?" I asked.

"Shut up, Walleski. Let's cut to the chase. Give me your story." He twisted in his seat and eyed me while he pulled out a pack of cigarettes and shook one free. Lighting it, he took a deep drag and blew the smoke toward me.

I inhaled and groaned. "Hey, can I bum one of those?" I asked, leaning forward and gazing hungrily at the pack he'd laid on the dash. He offered me the pack. Greedily, I snatched one out before he could change his mind. He lit it for me and tossed his lighter on the seat. I closed my eyes and felt I'd gone to heaven, as I drew in a lungful of smoke and held it.

"Well?"

I opened my eyes and exhaling in a rush, nodded. "Me and Connie, we got into it again. Had a doozie of a fight and I left. I knew I wouldn't be able to sleep, so I took a walk. To rethink a few things. Found myself out here and saw the snowman. Started looking for the missing nose and bingo, I found it. Didn't think it'd be in somebody's ear."

Dexter eyed me as he tapped ash from his cigarette out the window. "Didn't see anyone hanging around? Running away?"

"Nothing. Just me and the ice man."

Dexter glared at me and crushed out his smoke.

I savored mine, sucked on that baby 'til it was almost gone. I wasn't wasting a bit of that stick of gold.

Suddenly, the area was festooned with the bubble lights of emergency vehicles and the angry squawks of police radios. The troops had arrived. "Okay if I go?"

I said, pinching the last of the cigarette between my fingers. Couple more seconds, and it would burn me.

"Yeah, get out. I know where to find you." He jerked his head toward the door and laughed.

I glanced at the handle-less door. "I will, when you open the door." The burning butt seared my fingertips. I held my breath and counted to ten. *Hurry the hell up.*

Dexter came around and let me out. I dropped the butt like a hot potato and sucked on my singed fingers.

He laughed.

Asshole. I pulled out my cell and dialed my good friend Tack, a detective with the force. He answered and the sounds of a distant game of pool and clinking glasses muffled his voice. I knew where he was. The Hot Tamale, a local haunt we both frequented. I could hear Dave, the bartender, bellowing at one of his regulars. Yeah, bellowing. Picture a bull. Big thick neck and shoulders that barely clear the doorway— that's Dave.

"Cy, that you?" Tack's voice was clearer now and the sounds of the bar faded. I figured he had stepped outside.

"Yeah. You got a minute?"

"Sure. What's up?"

"I'm down at the old Pike place. I just found a body."

"You what?" I could hear Tack's heavy breathing across the line.

"You heard right. The Ten-Ten over the radio? That was me calling it in. I found a guy with a carrot stuck in his ear."

"Are you shitting me?" Tack's voice went up an octave.

"I walked here. Can you come get me?"

"Be right there."

I heard the click and buzz of the disconnect and snapped my phone shut. Now I'd just have to wait.

●●●●

I glanced down at my watch and was shocked to see it was after two. I was starving. Strange, considering I'd just discovered a body. My stomach started to growl. *Where can I get something to eat at this hour?* I thought of the little store I always went by. What was the name of it? Clover's Mini Mart. Yeah. I headed for the center of town and dreamed of a hot sub. Or pizza. *Tack will find me. He knows I can't stay still.*

It's a good thing I like to walk, I thought, slipping on a patch of ice, but then regaining my footing. I kicked at a cola can and watched it tumble in the wind.

My footsteps crunched as, deep in thought, I continued down Old Beach Road. That guy wasn't much more than a kid, and from the looks of his clothes, he hadn't been doing too badly for himself. Wasn't a local, and none of the guys had recognized him, either. I'd like to get another look at the body. Check the labels in his things. Maybe that would get the ball rolling to find out who he was. *Why was a stranger at the Pike place? And what was the significance of the snowman?*

Maybe Tack could pull some strings and help me get somewhere.

He used to be my partner in the good old days before the chief found out I was dating one of the key witnesses in a case, and kicked me off the force. I didn't use much smarts then, not that I do much better now, but at least I'm my own boss.

Clover's Mini Mart wasn't doing much business at 2:15 in the morning. A beat-up old Volkswagen bug, painted a hideous shade of green, sat partially covered by the newly fallen snow, and no other cars were in sight. As I walked through the door, the clerk looked up, glassy-eyed and yawning. He looked out of place, I thought, like a hippie leftover from the sixties. Long black hair hung almost to his waist, and some of those love beads hung around his scrawny neck. I could

5

feel his eyes follow my every move as I picked out a pizza from the freezer and grabbed a six-pack of Bud. I snagged a couple of Hershey bars at the register, too.

"How's it going?" I said, reaching into my back pocket for my wallet.

"Okay," he said. He glanced up at me with disinterest, as he finished ringing me up and started to bag my groceries. I swear a turtle could have gone faster. Once he was done, I thanked him and headed for the door. Behind me I heard a kind of grunting noise I interpreted as some form of you're welcome. Maybe in an alien language? Kids nowadays. I shook my head as I started down the icy steps. Lazy kid, couldn't even throw salt down.

I guess maybe I was a pain in the ass to all the adults when I was his age, but at least we'd had to have some kind of dress code when we went to work for somebody else. For crying out loud, he had on old ripped jeans that looked like they hadn't seen the inside of a washing machine in a long time.

The sound of a car pulling up beside me broke my ruminations. The warm air that belched forth from the interior as the window opened smelled of cigarettes and Drakkar aftershave. Tack leaned over and opened the door. "Hey, thought you were gonna wait for me?"

But hey, I've got to tell you about Tack. He always looks like he just stepped out of a men's fashion magazine. No kidding. No matter what time of day, there's Tack, looking like a Greek god. He's got an eye for great clothes and sexy ladies. Ah, maybe not in that order, but I guess you catch my drift.

The guys on the force used to joke with him about his choice of partners; after all, we were as different as night and day. But that's one thing I can say for Tack. He sticks up for his friends and I'm glad I can count myself as one of them. Even though I'm not one of the gang, Tack keeps me in the loop and helps me out when I need special favors. Like parking tickets. It helps to know somebody.

I pulled up the backseat and stowed my bags in the back, getting in the front. "Sorry about that. I had to have a snack. Knew you'd know where to find me. What's going on back at the Pike place? Heard anything?"

"Just the chief slinging insults and screaming about them messing up the crime scene. Seems everybody's been tromping through the snow, not being careful. Same bullshit. Different day." He tapped the bottom of a fresh pack of Marlboros, and I looked on hungrily. He shook one out and offered it to me. I grabbed it greedily and, with the lighter he offered, lit it. While I sucked on my cigarette like a hungry babe at its mother's breast, I watched him flick ashes out the window.

"Were you going to walk home with all that stuff?" he asked, motioning toward the back.

"Well, I wasn't gonna fly," I quipped. "Seriously, I could use the exercise, but it's damned cold out. Glad you came along."

"No problem."

The glow from the end of his cigarette was like a tiny beacon in the dark interior of the car. I leaned back and stretched out my legs toward the warmth blasting from the heater as we cruised down Willow Street and headed toward my house.

Chapter Two

Kent Blake twirled the beads around his neck, never taking his eyes off the man as he left the store. *Not a cop now, but had been.* He thought about his own arrival in town a few days before. It just so happened they had needed a clerk here at this place. Clover's Mini Mart: Where every visit is lucky. What a joke that motto on the wall over the door was. The job served its purpose, though. He needed cash.

Kent grew pensive, winding a strand of black hair, so like his mother's, around his finger. *I'm not leaving 'til I find that bastard and make him pay.* Hate bubbled up inside him.

He got back to the book he was reading. Flipping it open to the place where he'd left off, he shifted on his stool and escaped to the fantasy world of J.R.R. Tolkien.

●●●●

I looked around at the dingy walls and sighed. What a dump. Peeling paint, dents from my angry fist, ugly pictures from the fifties, and a mirror that had seen better days. I glanced at the weary stranger staring back at me. The once-black hair that all the girls loved to run their fingers through was now turning gray, and the body I used to be so proud of in college now sported a small paunch. A perpetual frown marred my features these days. There were only two things that nature hadn't taken from me yet. My six-foot frame and my blue eyes. I turned away from my hazy image and looked at the clothes that littered the floor, like discards on a lonely beach.

Mechanically, I began the process of what I call housecleaning. Groaning, I bent to pick up the clothes, shoving them into the cardboard box I referred to as a hamper. The bed was another story. My idea of making it was to pick up the blankets and fling them somewhere in the direction of the mattress. Empty beer cans on the bureau; evidence I'd slipped. Telltale ashes covered their tops and the sloshing contents held more than just stale beer.

Cursing at my weakness, I threw them into an empty paper bag I retrieved from under the bed. The cloud of dust that came with it threatened to block the sun for at least an hour. Carrying my soggy bundle, I went into the kitchen and dropped it into the trash.

If Connie were here she'd be cursing me out like crazy. "Cy, can't you clean up this mess? Get a real hamper for your clothes. What, are you smoking again? You drink too much." I miss the broad, what can I say? She keeps me in line. Without her, I fall right back into my old habits.

Time for the kitchen. Gathering up the paper plates from last night's *gourmet meal,* I realized I was hungry. Pizza for breakfast just didn't sound appetizing to me. I could go for a real breakfast. Fried eggs, bacon, home fries: the works. I grabbed my jacket from the back of a chair and headed for the door, turning back for my gun and a fresh pack of gum.

While I drove over to Sal's Breakfast Shack, I thought about last night's chain of events.

Early in the evening, I'd gone over to Connie's house to pick her up for dinner and a movie. She hadn't been ready. What else is new? So I'd wandered into the living room to wait. Cracking my knuckles to the rhythm of my gum-chewing, I'd watched a little boob tube. When she'd come out of the bedroom—looking pretty spectacular, I must say—she'd started in on

9

me. Why didn't I go back to the police department and work a real job? Why did I want to do PI work? What made me think I could write a book? How long did it take, anyway? When were we getting a place together? When were we getting engaged, at least?

"Damn it all!" I'd yelled, "Can't we just go out and have a nice quiet evening like other couples? Can't you even wait 'til I've had something to eat?"

"Fine. Go eat by yourself. I'm not hungry anymore!" she'd yelled in return, slamming the door as she went back into her bedroom, and that was that.

So I'd left. I'd started back to my apartment, feeling sorry for myself. *Is it so bad wanting to be my own boss?* I wasn't making millions, but I was putting food on the table and paying my bills. As far as my novel was concerned, I was working on it. It's slow going. *So, I'm not a bolt of lightning, what of it?* All this had gone through my head as I'd walked. Then my night had really turned to shit. I'd found that body.

I turned into Sal's parking lot and spotted a familiar sight, Tack's new-to-him Celica, its red paint glistening with just a touch of last night's frost. Pulling in beside his car, I was careful not to get too close. I knew how much he cherished that car.

Sal's place is great. It's a man's place. Nothing fancy. The outside is weathered shingles, like houses down the Cape, but not because Sal was trying to achieve that look. Oh no. Sal just never bothered to paint it.

Inside, it's kind of dark with a bunch of mismatched chairs surrounding equally odd tables. Still, the locals love it and gather here daily to hear the latest gossip, and eat some surprisingly good food.

I spied my pal sitting at our favorite table for two— by the band, I always joke. He motioned me over with his coffee cup. I took a seat. After a few minutes, Sal wandered over, coffeepot in hand, the perpetual butt hanging from the side of his mouth. For once, he didn't look too bad. He had on a clean, red-plaid flannel shirt and jeans, minus the usual grease stains. He's so damn tall and skinny he looks like a scarecrow. His black hair sticks out from the sides of his head, and his big beak of a nose makes him look corny. But he's not a bad guy, he just never has an awful lot to say. Like now.

"Usual, Cy?"

"Yup, and some pancakes. I'm starved."

With a curt nod, he filled my cup and headed for the kitchen.

●●●●

"What you got for me, Tack?" I asked, pouring a second half and half into my coffee. I stirred the swirl of white into brown and raised the cup to my lips. I looked at him over the rim. Sal slid a steaming plate to me and stalked off.

"The dead kid came from Florida," he said. He carefully cut into his omelet and took a bite. He picked up a slice of wheat toast, spreading jam on it. "Name's Clifton Blake. FBI," he said, taking a bite of toast.

"What the hell was he doing here?" I picked up a piece of bacon.

"Don't know yet. I'm working on it. Only thing on the body was his badge. He was for sure FBI."

I let this bit of information slowly digest and finished my coffee. Tack seemed to be off in his own little world, pouring himself another cup of coffee from the carafe. Stirring in sugar, he looked over at me. I knew what he was going to say. I beat him to the punch.

"It's weird. Nobody in town saw this kid or appeared to know him, yet he arrived here and got himself killed. At a deserted house in the middle of nowhere. But nobody saw anything!" I scratched the place on my chin I'd cut shaving that morning.

11

"No kidding. And no socks and shoes. That's crazy." Tack looked at me. I knew he was staring at the blood that had started to ooze from the nick on my chin.

I nodded. "I'm still thinking about the carrot thing. Why would anybody shove one in someone's ear? That's sick!" I picked up my napkin and dabbed at my chin.

"I got this." Tack reached for the check Sal had just dropped off. I handed Tack a ten, but he shook his head and jammed some bills under his cup. We waved to Sal from the door. The blast of cold air that greeted us was enough to take our breath away. At Tack's car, I waited while he disabled the alarm and got in. He lowered the window, lit a cigarette, inhaling sharply, and offered me one. "I'm gonna see what the FBI has to say."

I lit my cigarette with his lighter and nodded. I drew the smoke deep into my lungs, exhaling with a whoosh, blowing smoke upward. "Keep me in the loop, huh?"

He nodded. "We're pretty short-handed right now. Might need some help. You game?"

"Sure. Let me know." I watched as he spun out of the lot, fishtailing on the ice. I shook my head and ambled over to my old Toyota. *Time for a paint job for this old girl.* In some spots, the paint was so dull you couldn't see her true color, and, to tell you the truth, I couldn't remember what it was. Gray or blue. I brushed away a few errant flakes of paint by the driver's door. Poor old thing. Ah, hell. She always starts. "Well, old gal, home to clean." I'd spoken aloud and a couple getting into a little Nissan looked over and smiled. *Probably think I'm nuts.* I got into my car and started her up. The purr of her dependable engine made me smile, as I put her into gear and headed home.

Chapter Three

Dexter Phillips clenched his teeth. It was the rage. The same rage that had first come over him in Vietnam. It happened sometimes, out of the blue. It would take over, shutting everything else out. He'd been by himself that long-ago day, pushing through the jungle to take a leak, when he'd stumbled upon a small enemy camp. Being the big guy that he was, he'd made enough noise to alert them to his presence. They'd come after him.

Then the unthinkable had happened. He'd been hit with an incredible burst of hatred, so strong it had taken over and given him the surge of adrenaline he'd needed. Coming out from behind the trees, he'd cut all six of them down in a hail of gunfire. For that he'd received the Silver Star. For killing people.

Afterward he'd been in shock, horrified that he'd taken six human lives. But he'd learned to live with it. They all did, back then. That was another place and time. Something had snapped in him that night, and now he had to relive it, over and over in his head, for the rest of his life.

Dexter ran his fingers through the lengthening crew cut that he'd been meaning to have trimmed. Looking at himself in the rearview mirror, he saw his eyes—bloodshot and glassy. He looked like shit. He pulled into Clover's. Better get a coffee, if he was going to make the rest of his shift. Three more hours. Sleep was what he really needed.

The first snowflakes hit the windshield with a distinct ping. Dexter looked out the side window at what seemed to be the start of a nasty storm. "Shit. Just my luck."

●●●●

Hauling the big box down from the attic, I wondered why I always waited 'til the last minute to put up the tree. Here it was December twentieth, and I was just getting around to decorating. *Why the hell do I bother? There's just me, and not many people come to this dump to visit me. Can't say I blame them.*

Carefully unpacking the ornaments, I hung them here and there on the tree after stringing up the lights and the garland, and stood back to admire it.

I went out to the kitchen for a cold one and popped the top. Back in the living room, I sank into my easy chair and turned out the overhead lights to get the full effect. There's nothing like a good old-fashioned New England Christmas . . .

●●●●

I was ten again, gazing with wondering eyes at the tree we'd all carefully decorated. I thought it was the prettiest one yet. Ma, Dad, my two brothers and me had gone out to the woods on our farm and the folks had let us kids select, then cut down, what we thought was the best tree in the whole world.

This year, I hoped Santa was going to bring me a Flying Saucer. All the kids had them except me. I hated having to use a piece of waxed-down cardboard to slide down the hill behind our house. When Christmas morning arrived, I couldn't wait to run downstairs to see if Santa had really read my letter and brought that saucer. Opening the door to the living room, I shouted with glee, racing to the tree to pick up and inspect the shiny silver saucer. *Santa really does exist,* I remembered thinking on that long-ago Christmas. He really did.

14

●●●●

Chugging some more beer, I looked at the tree and felt a certain satisfaction. It really didn't feel like Christmas without one, not that I was feeling the spirit or anything, what with a dead body practically on my doorstep.

There hadn't been a murder in Gammil's Point, Maine since 1952 when Pat Fuller got drunk and shot his own son, who was just as drunk as his old man. No one really knew what the argument had been about, but Mrs. Fuller, still to this day, insists it was self defense.

People in town were walking around on eggshells back then, and I couldn't blame them. There was a killer walking in our midst. It's a shame when you can't even feel safe in your own home. Everybody locked their doors, warning their children not to talk to strangers, and peeking out from behind curtains at every sound.

This is a small town where everybody waves at you when you head uptown for a loaf of bread and a dozen eggs. It's just the way it is in small towns in New England. Folks stop to talk to a neighbor about the new baby. Old men meet at the doughnut shop and gossip about the fellow who just about lost his shirt at the casino, and who won the football game last week; the Patriots or the Dolphins. This is what small towns are like. But things had changed, turning Gammil's Point into a place where even snowmen weren't safe.

●●●●

The going was rough, roads slick with heavy snow, and visibility was next to nothing. Dexter leaned forward, peering out the windshield, trying to see the snowman in the growing storm. Each swish of the wipers pushed away a newly formed curtain of white. Hands tightening on the wheel, his knuckles whitened with the effort.

15

Suddenly fishtailing, he cursed, turning into the skid, the car careening forward. A telephone pole appeared out of the swirling storm, and Dexter braced for the impact. At the last moment, the car veered slightly to the left, sending the pole just out of the path of his car, which came to rest in a snow bank. He leaned back and closed his eyes, exhaling sharply, marveling at his near miss. Feeling his face redden, Dexter rubbed his sleeve across the window, staring through the glass to assure himself he was alone. One look in the rearview mirror showed nothing but white. He shifted into reverse, surprised when the car backed up effortlessly. The car's headlights cut through the driving flakes, glinting off the frozen form just ahead.

He'd been closer than he thought. Steering carefully to the side of the road, Dexter left the car running with only the parking lights to reveal its whereabouts.

Trudging through the deepening snow, he realized how bad this storm was getting; sure to get worse as the night wore on. The going was difficult, six or seven inches of the white stuff already covered the field. When he reached the snowman, he turned on the tiny flashlight he'd brought, aiming it at the snowman's head. The features were obscured by snow, except for the replacement carrot nose that poked out. Dexter reached out and grasped the carrot, tugging to pry it loose. It broke free from its icy home. He dropped it into his coat pocket, switched off the light, and headed back to the car. After a few steps, he stopped and went back. He pulled out another carrot from his pocket, similar in size to the one he'd just retrieved, and stuck it in the empty socket where the other one had been. Good as new. "Merry Christmas, Frosty," he said aloud, in the swirling snowflakes. "Catch you later."

A shadow detached itself from a nearby tree and watched Dexter get in his car and drive away. Nodding, the figure put his hands in his pockets and slogged through the snow toward the obscured path of his earlier footprints. He knew Dexter was up to no good, but what was he doing out here with a snowman?

It was just his great good fortune he'd been out here looking for a Christmas tree. He shook his head, hunching his shoulders up against the cold. What was he thinking, walking all this way from town instead of driving? His steps were muffled by the snow that was falling, and visibility was fast going from bad to worse. He let out his breath in a rush when he saw the winking lights from town. *Wouldn't want to get lost in a snowstorm around here. It could be days before anyone found you; then it might be too late.*

The sight of Clover's had never looked so inviting. Stumbling through the door, he welcomed the burst of warm air that enveloped him. He pulled off his damp gloves, rubbing his chilled hands. Coffee. Hot coffee. *A cup would be perfect right now.* He shuffled to the back of the store where a coffee maker, microwave and soft drink machine were located. A full pot of java sat on the burner. Hoping it was fresh, he took a paper cup from the stack and helped himself. He inhaled the aroma and, taking a sip, realized it was.

Dexter shut the door, but not before a swirl of snow had settled on the floor. He stamped his feet to the rhythm of the song still playing in his head. Taking off his coat, he hung it on a hook by the door and sat on the hall bench to pull off his boots. He tugged at the knotted laces, cursing when he couldn't loosen them, remembering what the clerk at the store where he'd bought them had said. "These laces will never give you trouble." *Where the hell is that knucklehead, so I can kick his ass?*

Finally freed of the cumbersome footwear, he padded to the kitchen and rummaged around in the fridge until his fingers touched cold metal. Just what the doctor ordered. He popped open the beer and took a deep draft. Rubbing a hand across his mouth, he grabbed a bag of Fritos from the cabinet beside the sink and headed for the TV. He passed his coat, held the bag of chips with his teeth, and reached into the pocket 'til his hand closed on the frozen carrot. He pulled it free, ambled into the living room and sank into the recliner in front of the TV. He put his beer on the floor beside him, took the bag from his mouth. The end of the carrot popped off easily. Dexter shook the contents onto his palm. Four of the biggest stones he'd ever seen winked up at him.

●●●●

Leaving his room at the Gammil's Point Bed and Breakfast, Kent Blake walked down Main Street headed for the house where Mrs. Shepherd, the owner, had told him he could find Dexter Phillips. The darkness was absolute at 8:30, but Kent liked it that way. He wanted to take the man by surprise. It was eighteen years too late; eighteen years was a long time for hate to fester like an open wound, and Kent felt like he was ready to explode. He stomped through the snow, closer to the house where his father lived. He clenched his fists.

Finding the house was easier than he'd thought. He crunched up the walkway to the door of 149 Windswept Lane, a typical New England Cape. The outside light that glowed beside the front door showed weathered shingles with white trim, and a dingy blue door in need of paint. Kent saw a car parked in the drive. He rang the bell and waited. A big man with cold, blue eyes and a crew cut flung the door wide.

18

Kent glared into the eyes of the man he hated more than anything else in the world.

"Can I do something for you, kid?"

"You haven't done a damn thing for me in eighteen years, so I guess you sure as hell aren't gonna start now, are you, *Dad?*" The last word was spit from Kent's lips with such venom he could almost taste the poison in his mouth.

Kent watched as the man's eyes widened. The big man advanced on Kent, who stood his ground, never flinching.

"What the hell are you talking about, kid? I never laid eyes on you before. I think I'd know if I had a kid!"

"Does the name Simone Blake ring a bell?" Kent snarled. "'Cause she's my mother and she says you're my old man!"

⬤●⬤●

Damn, it's cold in Maine. Kent strode from the house where he'd just delivered his bombshell. He smiled, thinking about the look on that dumb shit's face. He stuffed his hands in the pockets of his old leather jacket, head down against the cold wind that was biting at his face with such force it took his breath away. The snow stung his cheeks, wetting his face like tears. He turned back toward the bed and breakfast.

Tomorrow, he thought, *I'll go to the police station and nose around. See what I can find out about the old man.* Satisfied that he had a plan for the next day, he turned and headed to Clover's for some snacks.

●●●●

Kent picked up a basket at the door and toured the junk food aisle. He tossed Twinkies and Ring Dings in the basket. *Cheetos added to the mix would tide me over 'til the next meal,* he thought, yawning widely. He glanced at his watch and headed for the checkout. Candy Karroll worked the night shift most of the week. He was fascinated with her long hair; he stood staring at her blond mane which hung halfway down her back. She slowly picked up, then scanned, each item.

"That it?" she asked, smiling shyly, a dimple denting her left cheek. She twirled a strand of hair as she watched him.

"Yeah," Kent said. He handed her a twenty. "You working tomorrow night?"

She shook her head. "You?"

He nodded. He felt his face grow hot with the start of a blush, grabbed his bag and fled.

●●●●

Dexter stirred the pasta one more time, fishing out a single strand and blowing on it. He dangled it over his open mouth, savoring the fact that he'd actually gotten it right this time. *Al dente. Perfect.* He shut off the gas, emptied the spaghetti into a colander and ran a little cold water over it. Going back to the stove, he stirred the tomato sauce, scooping up a taste on the spoon. *Delicious.* He fixed himself a plate, complete with grated Romano cheese, and headed for the living room. An old rerun of Bonanza was starting, one of his favorites. Settling comfortably in his recliner, he reached for the glass of milk he'd brought in earlier and took several large gulps. *Tonight it's just Little Joe, the guys, and me,* he thought.

What a fucked-up day. Who the hell was that crazy kid, he wondered as he finished the last of his pasta. *Could I possibly have a kid? What else is Simone hiding from me?*

He watched the ending credits for *Bonanza* roll by and shut off the TV. The soft ping of snow was hitting the window, the glow from the streetlight shining in on him. Dexter looked out at the storm, watching as the wind picked up and blew swirls of white across the yard. Then he heard the clock chime ten and jumped to his feet, startled to realize he'd been dozing. He picked up his empty glass and plate and headed to the kitchen for some dessert.

As he rummaged in the fridge, pushing aside a half-empty jar of pickles, Dexter felt his resolve drain away like money in a slot machine. Could the kid really be his? Somehow he'd have to try to get through to the kid. Make it up to him. Let him know it wasn't like he knew about him, either. But until he could think of a way to do that, he'd have to tread lightly. That kid was one loaded gun just waiting for the right target, and Dexter didn't want to be the bull's-eye.

●●●●

Kent stepped into the phone booth, lifted the receiver and dialed the familiar number. After three rings, he heard his mother's sleepy voice.

"Hello?"

"Hi, Ma. It's me."

"Kent, where are you? I've been worried sick. Are you okay?"

"I'm fine, Ma. I'm in Maine." He waited a moment to let this sink in before continuing. "Don't get mad, I . . ."

"Kent, stop this. You don't know what you're doing. You're playing with fire!"

"I have to do this, Ma. He's gotta pay for what he's done."

"No! Come home, Kent. He's dangerous. You don't know him like I do."

"I gotta go. I'll call you tomorrow. Bye." He could hear her still talking as he hung up the phone. Then, gazing out at the brilliant glaze of snow-covered cars, he shivered, pulled up his collar, and stepped into the frigid morning air. He turned up Main Street and headed for his ten o'clock interview with the Chief of Police.

●●●●

Chief O'Malley stood and shook the young man's hand.

"Have a seat, son. What can I do for you?" He sat down in the chair behind his desk and glanced at the third drawer down, thinking with longing of the bottle resting within. Reluctantly, he brought his eyes back to the kid seated before him.

This boy, Kent, looks like trouble, he thought, groaning inwardly. He fiddled with a paper clip, fingers wanting to be unscrewing the top off the Jim Beam that was calling his name. He licked his dry lips and tried to pay attention to what the kid was saying.

"I have some questions about one of your officers, Dexter Phillips."

O'Malley cleared his parched throat and tried to dredge up a smile. He needed a drink.

"What's this about?" He felt a tingle start in his throat. His fingers itched along with his nose. He had to get rid of this kid. O'Malley plucked at his graying mustache, never taking his eyes off the boy seated across from him. He remembered seeing him get off the bus from Boston sometime in the last few days. *Why the interest in Phillips?*

As if reading the chief's mind, Kent answered, "I'm doing a paper for college. Heroes of the Vietnam War. He's one of the guys I want to interview."

O'Malley watched the kid straighten in his chair and eyed the long hair, tie-dyed T-shirt and multiple necklaces, sizing him up. Punk. "First of all, let's cut the crap. You got a Boston accent and I just so happened to see you get off the bus the other day." O'Malley leaned back in his chair and grinned. The kid's face had gone from one shade of pale to another. He could see fine beads of sweat dotting the kid's brow.

"Okay. You got me. Boston born and bred. Going to school there and I need to talk to Dexter Phillips.

In spite of what you think, I am doing a paper on war heroes."

O'Malley had to hand it to him, the kid was pretty slick. *Okay, two can play this little game.* His thoughts strayed back to the third drawer. He needed to get rid of this kid. He ran a hand through his thinning hair and caught a glimpse of himself in the mirror on the opposite wall. *When did I get so old? Where did those crow's-feet come from? And that nose. When did it broaden and turn a nasty shade of red?* He sighed and turned back to the kid from Boston. *What would it take to make him leave?*

Chapter Four

Slowing the cruiser, Dexter looked from side to side, trying to see through the growing twilight. He opened the window and aimed his flashlight at anything that moved, hoping to catch a glimpse of the small, elusive creature that he hunted.

"God damn it! Where the hell are you?"

Dexter pulled over to the side of the road, got out and mounted the snowbank. His boots pierced the crusty surface, the sound loud in the still air. He swung the light toward a noise off to his right. All he could see was the mound of snow lining the street, its surface peppered with dirt from the road.

"You have to be here somewhere. The old bag said this was where you jumped out." Mrs. Downs had called the station, sobbing that her beloved Snickers had escaped and she couldn't find him. O'Malley had gleefully given Dexter the job of finding the cat.

A timid meow sounded off to his right, a pair of glowing eyes appearing in the beam of his flashlight. "Here, Snickers. Nice kitty." Dexter pursed his lips and called to him, scrunching down on his haunches and reaching out to the small black and orange cat. "Come here, boy. I won't hurt you. That's it." Slowly the cat inched forward, mewing as he drew closer. Timidly, he crept up to Dexter's hand and delicately sniffed it, allowing Dexter to pat him. A sound to Dexter's left startled him, and the tiny cat fled into the woods.

"Shit!" Dexter spat. He pivoted to his left and started to rise. The barrel of a gun greeted him. "What the hell!"

The bullet pierced his tongue, exiting the back of his neck. He was dead before he hit the ground.

●●●●

I steered my car around a group of colorfully clad Christmas carolers strolling down the road, snatches of the songs they were singing drifting through the crisp night air. The reds, greens, and blues of their jackets added a cheery note to an otherwise gloomy night. I'd been feeling a little Scrooge-like with the thought of the big day looming, even as I, Mr. Always-Does-It-At-The-Last-Minute, groused about the fact that I hadn't bought a single gift yet. Hey, some of us work better under pressure, right? Well, that's what I always joked about, but, the fact is, I'm just not organized.

●●●●

The drive seemed to clear my head of any unwanted cobwebs of thought. I shook out a butt from the pack I kept in the car, put it in my mouth, and fished around in my pocket for my lighter—all the while keeping my eyes on the road, wary of any stray carolers who might have become separated from the group. My headlights brushed across something to my right as I rounded the corner. Sure enough, two dark figures trudged along, the narrowed beams from the flashlights they carried the only illumination in the frosty night. I lit my smoke and took a deep drag as I passed them, glancing in the rearview mirror. I thought I recognized Chub and Betsy Taylor.

I stopped the car, put it in reverse, and backed up to where they had stopped. I lowered the window, watching as Chub ambled over and leaned in the car.

"Hey, Cy, did you see a bunch of carolers headed for Main Street?" He rubbed his reddened nose and pulled his coat collar closed. Betsy came up to the car and smiled in at me, tucking some stray hair back beneath the red knit cap she wore.

"Yeah, I did. Hop in. I'll give you a ride," I said, motioning them into the backseat. Chub didn't seem eager to accept my offer, but Betsy hopped right in, slamming the door shut behind her. With a quick look at his shivering wife, Chub gave in, pulling the passenger door open and heaving his bulk in beside me. I reached over, turned up the heat, and turned the car around before they had even finished settling themselves.

"Pretty damned cold tonight, huh, Cy?" Chub rubbed his hands together and blew on them, his gloves resting in his lap.

"Yeah, I'm glad it wasn't me out there." I glanced over at him. "What the hell are you fools doing out on a night like this? Couldn't you put it off for a night or two?"

"Nah, Mitchell's a stickler for his schedule and when he says his choir is goin' carolin', they're goin' carolin'." Chub's expression looked pained as he continued, "Says we aren't stoppin' 'til we hit all the houses on the list. There's ten and we've only done three."

"The guy's got to be insane. It can't be more than ten degrees out there," I said, chancing a quick glance in my rearview mirror. Betsy looked like she couldn't walk another step, much less brave the frigid weather for seven more stops.

"I think you should quit and get some hot cocoa into your wife. She looks frozen. Hot showers wouldn't hurt, either." I glanced at Betsy again and she nodded. Chub looked ready to give in.

"Look, Chub, at least let me take Betsy home. She doesn't look like she can take much more." I jerked my thumb in her direction, hoping Chub would be sympathetic to his young wife. Nodding, he relented.

"Yeah, you're right, Cy. It's just too damned cold, but could you take us back to the group, so I can tell 'em we're goin' home?"

"Sure." I'd no sooner gotten the words out of my mouth, than I spotted the singers. By the looks of the group, others had already left, so the Taylors wouldn't be the first.

I pulled up beside them and a tall figure broke from the others, coming slowly toward the car. Mitch Cahill's long pointy nose was red from the cold, eyes watering as he dabbed at them with a wadded-up tissue. I lowered my window.

"Hey, Mitch. Don't you think you ought to call it a night? These two have had it." I jerked my thumb toward my passengers.

"I guess I don't blame you guys," he said, looking first at Chub, then Betsy. He stopped to blow his nose. "I think you're right. It's too damned cold." He shivered, stuffing his hands in his coat pockets, only to pull them out again and yank down the red and green striped stocking cap that perched high on his head.

"I can fit a couple of the ladies in if they want a lift back to the church or home," I said, motioning toward the stragglers hunched together. Cahill nodded and waved to them. Two women detached themselves from the others and hurried to the car. Under the watchful gaze of Cahill, the women squeezed into the back seat with Betsy.

"Okay, Cy, thanks for the help. I'll tell the others we're heading back." He nodded to me, and I watched him rejoin them, motioning toward my car. With a wave of his gloved hand, he herded them back toward town. I put the car in gear and started down the slippery road.

"Thanks for the ride. I'm frozen. Like that snowman." The speaker, a plump woman I recognized from somewhere, pointed at a lone figure in the field of the deserted Pike property we passed. The other lady who'd joined us just burrowed deeper into the puffy down jacket she wore, silent as the new-fallen snow.

"What the . . ." I stopped abruptly, fishtailing, sending Chub crashing into the door. I hoped it wouldn't fly open, sending the fat slob out on his ass. I shifted into reverse and backed up to the spot where we'd seen that snowman. A little cat crouched beside the figure, a lonely sentinel. I threw the car into park and turned to my passenger. Chub held his elbow, groaning.

"Sorry, Chub. You okay?"

"Dunno, Cy. Could be broke." The freckles on his pale face stood out like raisins in cake batter, his breath coming in sharp gasps.

"Think you can hang on a minute while I check this out?" I looked at the big man who rubbed his injured arm. He nodded. The women crowded against Betsy, trying to get a better look. That's when one of them screamed. I turned in my seat and saw why. In the moonlight, a human eyeball gazed out at us from the snowman's white face.

Kent jammed the gun into the waistband of his jeans, pulling his fleece jacket down over the telltale bulge. It had been a lot easier than he thought it would be, killing a man. He slogged through the snow, enjoying the buzz of adrenalin that still coursed through his veins. That asshole wouldn't be bothering his mother ever again. He smiled, remembering the look of surprise on the big man's face just before the gun went off.

The sound of sirens pierced the night air. Kent surged ahead, reaching a thick group of pines that huddled like dark sentinels in the still night. The wind whispered through their branches, snow swirling in the air. He tugged the black stocking cap he wore over his ears and stopped to listen. No sounds of pursuit, only the hoot of an owl greeted him. He was home free.

$$\bullet\bullet\bullet\bullet$$

Officer Punchillo, Punch to all the guys on the force, unfolded his almost seven-foot frame from the cruiser and strode my way. His eyes swept the scene, coming to rest on me and my new pal, the one-eyed snowman. It was lit up out here like a used car lot, and crime scene people scurried about like ants, while someone barked orders and the strobes of the units flashed like a blue-light special.

"What have we got here?" Punch asked, circling me and my frozen companion. He stopped and bent to examine the eyeball that protruded from the snowman's face. "Where's the rest of the body?"

"Over there." I pointed to a bunch of evergreens where a lot of the action was going on. Some of the personnel hovered not far from us, a few jotting down notes.

He cocked his head in the direction of the trees. "Know him?"

I nodded. "One of your own. Dexter Phillips."

His face lost what little color it did have. "Phillips? What the hell was he doing out here?

"Beats me. But he took a bullet to the head."

"And someone gouged out his eyeball?"

"Looks that way." I glanced at the eye, which was starting to get a frosty film on it. A technician came our way, excused himself, and stepped closer to the snowman, camera poised for another shot of the gruesome figure.

"Okay, people, let's wrap this up!" O'Malley slogged through the snow, coming our way. "Get that body out of here, and don't forget that eyeball!" he shot back over his shoulder to the knot of officers he'd just left. Their groans floated across the night air.

"You can go, Walleski. We know where to find you." O'Malley nodded at me. I turned to go.

"Hey, Cy. Good to see you. Sorry it's under such bad circumstances." Punch clapped my shoulder.

"Same here, Punch." I headed back to my car.

●●●●

Kent let himself into the darkened house with the key he'd taken from Dexter's pocket. Cupping his hand around the front of the flashlight, he headed for the staircase and the bedroom he assumed he'd find at the top of it. He reached the top of the stairs and padded down the hall to look into the first room, which was crammed with boxes and overflowing with junk. He shook his head and continued on. Next one down had to be it. An unmade bed that looked like someone had just gotten up from it dominated the small room. Kent eased inside and closed the door. Dirty clothes littered the floor, and the top of the bureau was crammed with bottles of aftershave. Something orange was lying on the pillows of the bed. Kent stepped closer for a better look, aiming his light on it. A carrot. He dropped the flashlight onto the bed and picked up the carrot. He noticed the end was scored. Sticking his fingernails into the grooves, he pulled the end free and shook the carrot. Two of the biggest diamonds he'd ever seen fell into his open palm.

●●●●

I'd never set foot in Dexter Phillips' house before today. A small but neat ranch, it was set back from the street a couple hundred feet. The walk leading to the front door was partially filled with drifted snow, footprints marring the otherwise perfect surface. As I made my way to the door, I felt the first flush of a panic attack. *Wonder what O'Malley wants?*

The front door opened and a uniformed cop stuck his head out, his gaze coming to rest on me. "Chief wants you." He beckoned me inside.

I entered the warm interior, the sound of the furnace kicking on in the background. Suits were weaving in and out of the downstairs rooms, some carrying evidence bags, some with other items they'd gathered from the house. Everyone was doing something, even O'Malley. I saw his smile fade as he came toward me, a large paper bag in his hands.

"Walleski, what took you so long?" He opened the sack and held it out for me to look inside. "Lookee what we got here." His smile was grim. "Think we know where these came from, right?"

The bag held a pair of men's shoes and socks. I leaned in closer and saw a billfold tucked beside the shoes. "The body from the other day? What the hell was Dexter doing with this stuff?"

"Don't know."

My eyes flicked toward the wallet he now held in his gloved hands. I watched him pull out a license.

"Yeah. His wallet, all right. Clifton Blake." He handed me the license.

I knew someone back in college with the last name of Blake. Simone. A girl I'd dated briefly before graduation.

"Weren't you romancing some dame with that last name?" He watched me intently, a smirk on his face.

I nodded. "Nice girl. We didn't hit it off. She was ready for the altar; I wasn't. End of story."

O'Malley chuckled. "I seem to recall she dropped that last name back in the day?" He watched me intently, a smirk on his face.

I nodded.

"She was out just before graduation. Wasn't knocked up, was she?"

"Look, let's get back to the present, okay? The past is over and done with. Can't do anything about it now, so let's forget it." I dropped the license back in the bag. I could feel my temperature rising with every dig O'Malley shoveled my way.

He handed the evidence bag off to a young officer who stood nearby, fiddling with his cell phone. The kid gulped loudly and, clutching the bag, shoved his phone out of sight in his back pocket. He nodded at his senior officer and scurried from the room, evidence in tow.

"Are you asking me to be a part of the team again?" I looked at O'Malley. His eyes seemed to bore right through me.

"I know you and I never saw eye to eye, Walleski, but it doesn't mean I don't value your input. Pressure from above made me cut you loose. Wasn't my idea. You're a damn good cop."

I almost fell over backward. *Did I hear right? Was O'Malley actually apologizing?*

"I want you to head to Boston. See what you can find on that Kent Blake, the kid who works at the Mini Mart. Came to see me, asking about Dexter."

"Does this mean you're hiring me back?" I leaned against the doorjamb.

"That remains to be seen. Do this and I'll see what I can do." With that, he turned on his heel and strode out the door.

●●●●

Kent let himself out the back door and headed through the woods, his boots crunching down into the thick crust of snow. He patted his jacket pocket, making sure his booty was still there. A smile crossed his face as he felt the reassuring bulge of the stones, hard against his palm. Something had made him take the carrot, too. Pulling on his gloves, he chanced turning on the flashlight for a moment. Ahead the trees thickened, the darkness swallowing him as he made his way deeper into the woods. He thought about the reason he'd gone to Dexter's house in the first place. He'd thought maybe he'd find a bunch of cash stashed somewhere. He hadn't found money, but what he had found was a lot more valuable. Kent chortled. The sound echoed in the still night air. *Tomorrow we'll see just how rich I'm going to be.*

●●●●

I made my way back to the car, breath coming in big puffs. While I'd been inside Dexter's house, the temperature had dropped considerably and the thought of a warm car, heat belching from the vents onto my cold feet, made me pick up the pace. Once inside, I checked the temperature gauge. Cold. While I sat there waiting for the engine to heat up, I rubbed my chilled hands together, thinking about the dead boy I'd found. An FBI agent from Florida and a Boston kid with the same last name. *Coincidence? Why was the FBI here?*

And what's up with O'Malley? Why the change of heart? It's not as if he really likes me. I shook my head and turned on the heater. Blessed warm air blew down on my frozen feet, and I wiggled my toes, thanking the heater gods. I switched on the radio and turned up the volume. Bing Crosby was singing his heart out about wanting to be home for Christmas. I couldn't help but smile, in spite of the somber tone of the night. Tomorrow I'd head to Boston and try to find Kent Blake's family.

Chapter Five

Colored lights were tacked around the picture window of Sal's Breakfast Shack, giving the place a festive glow. A large plastic Santa blinked on and off, greeting the new arrivals at the door. Inside, a cheap-looking artificial tree claimed the left back wall, its branches covered with red and gold balls of various sizes, lights twinkling. Beneath the tree, gaily wrapped packages sported big red and gold bows. *Sal outdid himself this year,* I thought, *or he actually allowed Martha to come in and decorate the place.* Either way, it sure looked cheerier.

I headed for my usual spot. Picking up the coffee cup, I turned it over and waited, a signal that always brought either Sal or Martha, coffeepot in hand. I glanced around the room to see who was in today. Chub Taylor sat in his usual spot, a stack of pancakes holding his attention. His nickname suited him. At about three hundred pounds, with an ass as broad as a battleship and a belly to match, he was a force to be reckoned with. Hell, you could paint him gray and float him in the harbor. He'd make a hell of a good target. If I didn't know any better, I'd swear he was sitting on air, his buttocks blousing over the chair, hiding all but the legs. The few strands of pale red hair he had were combed across his balding pate, and the freckles on his balloon-like hands stood out in sharp contrast on his colorless skin.

At the table next to him, Clay Dickerson sat staring into his coffee cup, a plate of uneaten toast before him. Pauline, his wife of fifty years, sat opposite him, pushing scrambled eggs around her plate with her knife. The expressions on their wrinkled faces were strained. Their frequent battles were a constant source of town gossip. Clay was a drinker. I'd heard she did her fair share, too.

"Hey, Cy. Where you been?" Sal's homely face broke into a grin that reminded me of a jack-o'-lantern. I turned to face him, surprised to find he was actually quite in the spirit himself. He wore a bright red shirt, his usual jeans, and a pair of green-and-white-striped suspenders. A Santa hat perched on his wild hair. I had to laugh at the sight.

I held out my cup, almost dropping it when Sal started cackling. I think it was the first time I'd heard him laugh. "Like my duds, huh, Cy?" he asked, watching me closely.

"Sal, you never cease to amaze me."

"Well, I figured it being so close to Christmas and all, I'd better get into the spirit, at least a little, ya know, to get the customers in a good mood. Good for the tips."

"You crack me up, Sal."

"Yeah, I know, a regular comedian." He guffawed. Growing serious, he pulled out a dirty-looking pad of paper. "Ready to order?"

"Pancakes today, Sal. Blueberry. Chub seems to be enjoying them." I nodded in his direction.

"Okey dokey."

He ambled off toward the kitchen while I stirred cream and sugar into my coffee. Taking a swig, I cursed under my breath. I'd just burned my tongue. Absently, I twirled my spoon around on the table. I was still thinking about Dexter's eyeball on that snowman. The fact that he'd been killed by a service piece didn't sit right with me, either. Who the hell wanted the big man dead?

The smell of blueberries brought me back to the present. Sal plunked a plate of steaming pancakes oozing with blueberry juice on the table in front of me. I licked my lips in anticipation. Sal stood there a minute, watching as I took my first bite. He nodded and went off to check on the Dickersons. I doctored up my second cup of coffee and took a cautious sip. Just right, this time. I was so into my meal that it took me a minute before I realized someone was hovering over my shoulder, breathing heavily. I turned and looked up to find Chub eyeing me expectantly.

"Hey, Chub. How's the arm?" I asked, nodding toward his ham hock of a shoulder.

"Ain't broke, but the doc says rest it a couple days. Sure is sore, though." He rolled his shoulder and winced. "See what I mean?"

I watched him, thinking that he looked like a circus elephant waiting for his next cue. He had a smear of blueberry juice on his right cheek.

"Hey, Cy. What you hear about that dead guy you found?" He didn't wait to be invited, pulling out the chair opposite me, carefully lowering his bulk down onto it.

"Not much, Chub. Just what's in the papers." I wasn't about to tell him anything. He'd broadcast it all over town. I watched him plunk his coffee cup down on the table. *Shit. He can't be deterred.*

"How're things going with you and Connie?" he asked, taking a gulp of his coffee.

"Right now, I'm in the doghouse." I said, taking another bite of my pancakes. I pushed around another piece on my plate, making sure to sop up all the blueberry juice. I never leave a drop of those babies.

"Hmm. Too bad, Cy. Ah, women. Betsy's always threat'nin' to go home to mama, if I don't lose some weight. Know what I tell her? Go ahead. I can live without ya. Maybe I'd get a little peace for a change instead of her always yappin' at my heels." He reached up and scratched his chin.

I turned away, not wanting to lose my appetite this early in the day. Chub wasn't what you'd call a class act.

"Women. Can't live with 'em. Can't live without 'em." He laughed heartily, his shirt riding up to reveal his stretch-marked belly.

Martha suddenly appeared at my elbow, a little gray mouse of a woman, her dishwater-blond hair done up in a bun on top of her head. She wore a bright red sweater, little green blinking ornaments hanging from her ears. She filled our cups, nodding to me.

"Hi, Martha."

She glanced nervously in Sal's direction. "I saw that man in here the other day," she said, motioning with the coffeepot at the picture on the front page of the paper Chub now held. "He was asking all kinds of questions." She glanced Sal's way again.

"What? The dead kid?" I snatched the paper from Chub's meaty hands. I spread it out on the table and studied the young man's face staring back at me. "You sure?"

Martha nodded. "I never forget a face. Especially such a nice one." Her smile seemed to melt, eyes darting back and forth. "I gotta go." She clutched the coffeepot and scurried off.

"I was in here that day," Chub said, nodding vigorously. "Saw him, too." He jabbed a sausage-like finger at the photo. "Real polite. Even talked to *me*. Can ya beat that?" He snickered.

"Hey, you gonna finish those?" he asked, pointing at my plate of half-eaten pancakes. I pushed it his way. Let the pig finish it.

"Did he say what he was doing here?" I asked, watching as Chub ran the back of his hand across his mouth. He belched loudly. I rolled my eyes.

"Nah. Just asked if there was someplace he could stay. I hooked him up. Sent him to Kathy's. She's got an extra room."

He'd been trying to hook me up with his cousin Kathy for the last three years. I watched him pour three spoons of sugar and half the cream pitcher into his fresh cup of coffee. I needed to get rid of him. And talk to Kathy.

"Still think you oughta consider Kathy, Cy. She's a good sort."

"I'm sure she's lovely, Chub, but one woman's all I can handle." I pushed back my chair and got up. I gave Sal a signal and he hurried right over. Thank God. He handed me the check and looked over at Chub, eyebrows raised. *I think I've had enough of a sideshow for one day.*

●●●●

Martha's hand shook as she took out a coffee filter and packet of coffee from the cabinet. She tore open the package, emptying it into the filter and shoved it in the machine, stabbing the start button. She took down a clean mug, spooned in sugar and sat down to wait.

Why didn't I tell Cy everything about that day? Can I risk it and phone him? Set up a meeting? Martha shook her head, fear twisting around her heart like an octopus' tentacle.

The strident ding of the kitchen bell startled her. She turned to see table number ten's order sitting under the warming lights, steam rising from the food, the aroma making her stomach growl. She realized she hadn't eaten all day and, glancing at the clock, was surprised to see it was after four.

Sal's voice made her jump. His footsteps were coming toward the service station where she frequently hid. Pouring her coffee with an unsteady hand, she risked a quick first sip. Rising, she hurried to deliver the food.

Chapter Six

Kent sat on his bed, mesmerized by the sparkling stones he held. In the early morning light, they looked even bigger than they had the night before. Where could he pawn them? He thought of his friend back home. Spike knew the streets and how to get around. A few years older, he'd spent some time in the slammer. One cool dude.

Dropping the diamonds into a paper bag, he picked up his cell phone and dialed his friend's number. Finally, after many rings, Spike's voice grated over the line, informing callers that he wasn't available and to leave their name and number and maybe he'd get back to them and maybe he didn't give two shits. Kent rolled his eyes. Typical Spike. Sick sense of humor. But he liked it.

"Hey, Spike. It's me. I got a proposition for you and maybe you will give a shit about this." He chuckled as he clicked off. Think I'll fuck with that asshole sheriff. Bring back that carrot.

●●●●

Driving down 95, as I headed into Massachusetts, I realized the roads were becoming less icy and the pavement was actually showing in spots. My car slithered a bit as I hit another patch of ice. I steered toward the skid and regained control as a semi passed me, horn blaring. I shot up my middle finger as his tires shot slush at my windshield. I turned on the wipers, slapping the mess out of my line of vision.

O'Malley had sent me on this jaunt with the promise he'd look into hiring me back. I figured finding information on a runaway kid should be easy. Kent Blake.

I pulled over at the next rest area and shook out a smoke. My fingers trembled as I held the lighter to the cigarette. Taking a deep drag, I held it in until I couldn't hold it any longer. Exhaling in a rush, I thought about the dead young man. Slight build, dark hair and light complexion. Could he and the clerk be brothers?

I crushed out the butt in the ashtray and headed back onto the highway, the rear end of the car skidding as I gave it a little too much gas. I eased up on the pedal and steered into the flow of traffic, yielding to the angry toots of drivers' horns as they passed me.

I smiled and gave them my customary salute as their slush hit my window.

Welcome to Massachusetts.

●●●●

It was a typical Friday in the big city, three days since I'd found that body. Traffic was a bitch and idling cars sat bumper to bumper on Commonwealth Avenue with yours truly smack in the middle. I lit up a smoke and opened the window. At quarter past eight, the streets were a mass of humanity, everyone heading to work like ants on their way to a picnic. I blew out a stream of smoke into the cold morning air and reached over to switch on the radio. Surfing the channels, I settled on an oldies station and leaned back.

My cell phone buzzed on the seat beside me. I reached over and checked the screen. Connie.

"Hey, babe. Still mad at me?" I said.

"I should be." I heard her sigh. "Where are you?"

"Cooling my heels in Boston traffic."

"Boston!"

"O'Malley sent me. I'll be home tonight unless things change."

"Can we talk when you get back?"

"Sure." I thought about all the other times we'd fought and gotten back together. *Was it really worth salvaging?* Maybe it was time to move on.

I heard ice clinking in a glass and imagined her sitting in her pink kitchen sipping a cocktail. Too much of that lately.

"Cy?" she whispered. "I'm sorry."

"Me, too, babe. Me, too." I closed my phone and tossed it on the seat.

Traffic finally started moving. I leaned over, peering through the window to find the address O'Malley had given me. *Kid must come from money,* I thought, looking at the brick fronts of the homes I passed. I found the place and double-parked out front. Fuck it. Let them give me a ticket.

Ringing the bell of number 290, I glanced around at the other homes. I wouldn't live here for all the tea in China. I stood there cracking my knuckles while I waited. Not a sound from the house, but a woman walking her little dog stopped on the sidewalk.

"Nobody's home." She frowned. "You a cop?"

"Private investigator, ma'am." I descended the stairs and flipped open my ID.

"I shouldn't be talking to you. None of my business." She gathered up her tiny dog in her arms and tramped through the dirty snow to the house next door. The door slammed shut. I watched a curtain in a front room be flicked aside by an invisible finger.

I sighed. *Maybe I'll try back later.* I pulled out my cell phone and scrolled through to my notes as I made my way back to the car where a city cop was giving me a present. I stopped and watched as he tucked the ticket under my wiper. Shit.

●●●●

Spike gingerly touched the latest additions protruding from his forehead and cursed. He was told it wouldn't hurt that much when he went to his friend's tattoo parlor to have two knobs placed under the skin to look like devil's horns. He looked in the mirror and cringed. His forehead was turning an ugly mottled purple and green where the new horns were. He fingered the rings that studded his lower lip and clipped a gold ring through his nostrils. Flexing his biceps, he liked what he saw. A large snake tattoo slithered down his right arm, and a realistic skull graced the left. He put his wallet in the back pocket of his skin-tight jeans and was reaching for his phone when it came alive.

The cell jiggled across the bureau as a heavy-metal song started playing. Spike groaned. The ringtone was the one he'd assigned for his friend Kent. What did he want now? He headed for the bathroom.

"What?" he growled into the phone.

"Yeah, hello to you, too. Didn't you get my message?"

"Maybe. What's so important? Hey, where the hell are you, anyway?"

"What, are you taking a piss while you're talking to me?"

"Hey, a man's gotta do what a man's gotta do," he chuckled, flushing the toilet.

"I got something I need you to do," Kent said.

"Yeah. What?"

"I need you to pawn something for me."

"Hey, what are you up to? You never answered me. Where the fuck are you?" Spike reached up to his forehead and gently rubbed the offending knobs. They ached like hell. He was sure gonna give Axel a piece of his mind when he saw him later.

"Maine."

"What? Are you outta your mind? I told you to let that go, man."

"That's old history now. You gonna be home?"

"Sure. Got nothin' better to do. Why? You comin' back?"

"On my way. Just got on the interstate. Meet me at the usual place," Kent said.

"Can't wait to see what's got your panties in a knot," Spike said. He flopped into a large stuffed chair in the living room and lit up a bone. "I'll be there." He smiled, took a deep drag, and ended the call.

●●●●

Martha pulled the hood of her parka up around her face and shivered. Just after three o'clock, the temperature had dropped by at least ten degrees. Sal had stayed behind to clean and set up for the morning, and she'd been relieved. She needed some time to think. Cy said he was heading to Massachusetts. Once home, should she chance phoning him?

The interior of the Ford was glacier cold. Her hands shook as she tried to start the car, the engine groaning in protest. Martha gave it some gas and revved the engine while she fumbled in her purse for her phone. She looked in the rearview mirror, shocked at what she saw. Her lipstick was a blood-red gash of color on the stark white palette of her face. She glanced down at her sweater peeking from her coat and realized she still wore her nametag. Sal would be pissed at her for not removing it.

Her fingers curled around the phone. She raised her head and glanced back at the restaurant. Would Sal miss her? Not wanting to chance him seeing her leave, Martha dropped the phone back into her purse and put the car in gear. She pulled out of the lot and nosed the car into traffic, careful not to go too fast. The road felt slick when she slowed for a red light. She lightly pumped the brake and glided to a stop.

She released the steering wheel, flexed her stiffened fingers, watching a tightly bundled figure cross the road in front of her car, blue scarf flapping in the wind. When the person reached the curb, Martha saw the first snowflake hit the windshield. She groaned. The light turned green and the guy in the car behind her laid on the horn. Martha gave him the bird and hit the gas.

◆●◆●

O'Malley lit a cigarette and leaned his office chair back on two legs. He kicked off his shoes and put his feet on the paper-strewn top of his desk. It felt good to relax. The folks in town were starting to get on his nerves. When you gonna catch this monster? What are you doing to find this guy? Shouldn't you call in the feds? He was sick of their questions and accusing looks. Who did they think he was? *Superman?*

Bringing the chair back down, O'Malley reached into the drawer and took out his salvation. Jim Beam. He pulled out the shot glass he'd brought home from Niagara Falls last year. Its cheery sentiment reminded him of another glass he'd found on a foray into Massachusetts years ago. That one was from Martha's Vineyard. O'Malley poured a generous dollop into the glass and downed it. He rubbed a hand across his mouth and refilled the glass. Again he swallowed the liquor, feeling it work its magic already, the familiar buzz caressing him like a lover.

O'Malley thought about the last few days. There was a killer on the loose in Gammil's Point, and one of his officers, Dexter Phillips, had been involved somehow. He thought about the night he'd followed Dexter to the old Pike place and watched him pull the carrot nose from that snowman and shake something into his palm. The contents had glittered in the moonlight and there'd been no doubt in his mind. Diamonds.

He rummaged in the top drawer and pulled out a set of keys. He frowned. Where the hell did those rocks go? They didn't find anything at Dexter's. He looked at the keys he held. Maybe those idiots who worked for him didn't look in the right place. Maybe he would. He smiled and reached for old Jim.

Chapter Seven

Was this going to be a wasted trip? I looked up at a gray sky that was just itching to start snowing. The fronts of the brick buildings seemed to mock me like a bunch of old women, laughing from their rocking chairs. Nobody home. That lady's voice echoed in my mind. A curtain in the front window of her home fell back into place. She was watching me again. I'd passed a little convenience store up the street. Maybe I could get some dirt there. I shot one last look at the nosy lady's house and pulled away from the curb. I gave a little wave out the window in case she was watching.

•◆•◆

The interior of the store was crammed with every imaginable thing you could ever want and then some. I meandered down the aisles, past hair curlers, cap guns, duct tape, and every magazine known to man. At the rear, a back room with a sign overhead read XXX. I wasn't even going there. I headed back to the front of the store and the young girl snapping gum as she tapped at the keys on her cell phone. Her long blond hair swayed to the rhythm of her fingers.

She looked up at me, smiled and blew a bubble. "Can I help you?" She didn't wait for a response, just went back to her texting.

"Are you busy or can I ask you a few questions?" I looked at the stuff on the counter and picked out a lighter from a display. I shoved it her way. "I'll take this."

Little Miss Bubble Head yawned and put down her cell phone. She eyed me warily. "Depends. You a cop?" She drummed her fingers on the counter, the neon orange polish on her nails bright in the gloomy interior.

"Not anymore. I'm a private investigator." I held out my ID for her.

She glanced at it and looked up at me. "What do you want?" She snapped her gum again.

"Do the Blakes come in?" She took the gum from her mouth and tossed it in the trash.

"Maybe. I don't do names." I studied her face. Nothing.

She shook her long curtain of hair and pushed a strand behind her ear.

"How about this woman?" I showed her an old snapshot of Simone. I'd dug it out before leaving, thinking it might come in handy. The girl peered at it, eyebrows furrowed.

"Sure. Could be a lady I see. Yeah, maybe." She shrugged.

Inspiration hit me. I took out my cell and brought up the gallery of photos I'd taken. I'd snapped a quick one of the kid in the store back home. I ran my finger over the tiny screen, called up the image, and held it out.

"How about this kid?" Her eyes widened. "Know him?" I said.

"Yeah. He's in all the time." She reached out and touched the picture.

"Been in lately?"

"No." She shook her head, hair swaying like seaweed. "Haven't seen him in a few days."

"Know his name?" I felt my breath catch.

"Ken, I think. I remember 'cause I thought he was kinda cute." She blushed. "They came in together. The lady in the picture and him." She nodded more vigorously. "I'm sure it was them."

47

"But you don't know their last name. Could it be Blake?"

She leaned on the counter, chin in hand and shook her head.

"Sorry. But he sometimes comes in with another guy. Spike. Real scary. Tattoos and tons of piercings. Everybody steers clear of him. I don't like to wait on him. When he looks at me, it's like he's seeing right through my clothes." She shuddered, wrapping her arms around herself.

I felt like I was finally getting somewhere. "Know where I can find this Spike?"

"Sure. Everybody knows. I'll give you the address, but don't tell him I gave it to you. He'd kill me." She ripped a piece of paper from a pink note pad and scribbled the address. She handed me the slip.

I nodded. "Thanks for your help, Bonnie." She looked startled. I pointed to her nametag.

She looked down, smiled, and nodded. "You're welcome."

I left the store and got back in my car. I adjusted the rearview mirror and saw the same woman I'd seen walking her dog approaching on the sidewalk. I waited to see if she recognized the car. She saw me watching her and scurried into the store.

●●●●

Martha used the side of her foot to sweep the snow from in front of the door. She let herself in and dumped her purse on the small table in the hall. The house felt cool to her and she hurried to check the thermostat. Just as she thought. Sal had turned the temperature down to sixty again. Damn him. She cranked it up to seventy-five and smiled.

Her stomach growled, reminding her she still hadn't eaten. She took off her coat and stepping back outside for a moment, shook the snow from it. She shivered. It was getting colder. Back in the house, she hung the coat in the hall and entered the kitchen. A cup of tea and maybe a sandwich. She filled the teakettle from the tap and placed the pot on the burner. She sat at the table and stared at the flames, thinking about the young man who'd been killed. Her eyes went to the black wall phone. Cy. She needed to call him. Tell him what she'd seen. As if sensing her thoughts, the phone started to ring. Martha jumped.

She gripped the edge of the wooden table and tried to rise on legs that suddenly felt like limp spaghetti. The phone kept ringing. She willed her legs to move and stumbled to answer it.

The voice on the other end of the line chilled her to the bone.

I'd maneuvered my way out of Back Bay and got on Mass Avenue, headed toward Dorchester. The address on the sheet of pink paper was in a less than savory neighborhood. Banged-up cars littered the streets like discarded candy wrappers. I licked my dry lips, not liking what I saw. The rusty-red three-decker where Spike lived was surrounded by a weed-choked yard with an old push-type lawn mower for decoration. I winced and pulled into what I took to be the driveway. I thought I saw someone peeking from a window on the first floor. I got out and approached the house, careful of where I stepped.

When the door opened abruptly, in answer to my knock, I was momentarily stunned, both by the movement and the sight that greeted me. Bright orange hair standing straight up in an exaggerated Mohawk topped a face permanently disfigured by the piercing of lips, nostrils, eyebrows and ears. His forehead had two nubs protruding from it, angry-looking incisions just below them, the skin an awful shade of purplish-green. Mini crosses of diamonds and little skulls with red jewel eyes hung from his ears like sports trophies.

After what seemed like hours, I closed my mouth. The creature that faced me scowled.

"Yeah? Who're you?" he spat around the silver stud in his tongue.

"Cy Walleski. Private detective." I flipped open my wallet so he could get a good look at my I.D. "You Spike?"

The devil-man backed up a few steps. "I got nothin' to say to no half-assed dick."

I pushed back my jacket showing him I was packing heat. "I just want to talk. About your friend Kent." His eyes flicked from my jacket to my face. The look he gave me could have stopped a rabid dog.

"Shit." He rubbed at the puckered skin of his forehead and motioned me in. I sidled in and tried to avoid brushing against his studded leather pants as I went by. He adjusted the matching vest he wore and jerked a thumb toward a room to our right. I followed him in.

The furniture in the sparse living room looked like someone's Salvation Army cast-offs. Two oversized armchairs and a couch belching stuffing sat opposite each other. Didn't look too clean. I lowered myself gingerly onto the sofa.

Spike sat opposite me on one of the ugly chairs and placed his booted feet on a worn mahogany coffee table that was littered with Dunkin' Donuts coffee cups. An overflowing ashtray completed the mess.

"Okay. Talk." Spike shook a cigarette from a pack of Marlboros he'd plucked from the debris on the table. I watched him finger a gold lighter, then light up his smoke. He blew a stream of smoke toward the ceiling.

"Nice place." I started to lean back, then thought better of it.

He grunted. "You from that shithole where he's at?" Spike took a deep drag and held it in.

The smell of the smoke was driving me crazy. I needed a cigarette. "Yeah. Gammil's Point."

"Whatever." He flicked ashes onto the floor. "What's he done?"

"Maybe killed someone." I watched his face.

"No shit." He crushed out the cigarette on the floor with the heel of his boot.

I glanced at the floor and watched a curl of smoke rise from the discarded cigarette. "I'd pick that up if I were you."

"Fuck off." He bent and picked up the butt, dropping it into the ashtray. He got up and advanced on me, jamming a finger into my chest. "Leave."

I, too, stood. I brushed his hand aside like it was a pesky fly. "Here's a message for your friend. He and I need to have a little chat. Got that?" I poked his chest with a business card I'd pulled from my pocket. "Take this. Give it to him. He's gonna need a friend."

"Whatever." He rubbed at the knobs on his head and glared at me. "Let yourself out," he snarled. He stalked from the room.

I saw a dirty pad of paper resting among the debris on the coffee table. I edged closer and tugged it free. Someone had doodled all over the top sheet. It looked like a bunch of diamonds and hidden within the rest of the scribbling I saw a name. Dexter Phillips. Why would Dexter's name be on a sheet of paper in this guy's house? Diamonds? I tore off the sheet, folded it, and tucked it in my pocket. I looked up at a noise from the front of the house. *I better leave before the freak comes back.* I slipped from the room and let myself out.

Chapter Eight

Chub hung up the phone and scratched his belly. He leaned back in the chair and thought about what Martha had just told him. She'd been out in the woods the night the body was discovered. Had she seen him?

Betsy bustled through the kitchen door and stopped short when she saw her husband.

"What are you doing home so early?" She dropped a package on the table and came closer. "Not sick, are you?" She reached out to feel his forehead.

"Nah. I'm fine." He slapped away her hand. "Where you been?"

"One last Christmas present." She nodded toward the bright package on the table. "Did you see Martha this afternoon? She looked awful. Like she was coming down with something." She filled the kettle and turned on the burner. Automatically she reached for two cups. "Tea?" At his silence she twisted back around. Chub's face was the color of chalk.

"What's wrong?"

"Nothing. I'm gonna lay down for awhile. Call me for dinner." He rose, gripping the table with both hands. "Don't make it 'til . . ." He looked at his watch. "Six."

Betsy eyed her husband as he lumbered from the room. She waited to hear his steps on the stairs before grabbing her cell from her purse. She hit the number on her contact list.

"Hello?"

"Martha?" she whispered. "You okay? You didn't look good this afternoon."

"It's nothing. I'm fine."

"Come on. We've been friends too long. I know you. Something's wrong."

"Betsy, leave it alone. I can't talk about it."

Betsy heard a click. The line went dead.

My phone started vibrating on the way back to my car. I waited 'til I got behind the wheel before I checked the screen. Didn't know the number. Maine exchange, though.

"Yeah. Walleski here. I could hear soft breathing on the other end.

"Cy? It's Martha."

"Hi, Martha. Everything okay?" I started the car and backed out of the drive, but not before I saw Spike round the side of the house, overnight bag in hand. I drove around a corner and pulled to the side of the road to wait for him to pass.

Martha's tremulous voice reined me back in. "I need to talk to you. About something I saw. I think it's important. It's about that boy who was killed."

"What?" I had half an ear on what she was saying while my attention was focused on the beat-up car that sped by me, Spike at the wheel.

"Can you meet me? At The Frosty Mug?"

"Can't right now. I'm in Massachusetts."

"Massachusetts?"

"I'll be home later. How's eight?"

She sighed. "I guess."

I heard a door in the background. "Gotta go."

The old clunker sped by me and I followed. The roads were slick and the other car threw wet slush back at my windshield. I turned on my wipers and smiled when I saw where he was going. The Southeast

Expressway, heading north. *Old Spike's heading to his friend's rescue. This could prove interesting.*

I punched in a station on the radio and turned the volume down low. Soft Christmas music filled the air, and I hummed to the tune. I hadn't gotten in touch with anyone at the Blake house, but this was even better. Spike would lead me back to where Kent was hiding, and maybe then I'd get some answers.

I spotted the car a few lengths ahead of me. He moved over to the slow lane and put on his right blinker. I eased into the same lane and prepared to follow. He was taking the next exit. What the hell was this kid up to? We'd only been on the road for twenty minutes. My wheels lost traction for a minute and I felt the car start to fishtail. I struggled to keep control. The tires grabbed the snow-covered pavement, and we were in business again. I realized I'd been holding my breath. I exhaled, wishing for a smoke.

The clunker slid onto the exit ramp with me far enough back so Spike, hopefully, wouldn't see me. I saw where he was headed. The familiar logo of Dunkin' Donuts beckoned from our right. I drove after him and stopped just shy of the parking lot. I watched him pull into a parking space. What now? My stomach started to growl. I envisioned a large coffee and an éclair, my mouth watering.

I turned off the car and waited. My patience was rewarded when not fifteen minutes later an old lime-green Volkswagen pulled into the spot beside Spike's. Bingo. *Has to be Kent.* Sure enough, the same longhaired kid from Clover's stepped from the VW bug and slid into Spike's heap. I smiled. *This keeps getting better and better.*

I shivered, drawing my coat closer around me. The interior of the car was steaming up from my breath and my feet were getting cold. I rubbed at a patch of frost on the windshield that obscured my view.

"Shit." The freak's car had disappeared.

●●●●

Chief O'Malley picked up the paper and scanned the day's headlines. *Never anything good to read in this hick town's rag.* He tossed it aside. His fingers itched to open the drawer and have a swig. Just one. Abruptly, he pushed back from his desk and got up. The coffeepot was full of fresh coffee his deputy had just made. He poured himself a cup and added a generous dollop of cream and a couple of sugars. He took a sip and grimaced. When would he learn? It just couldn't take the place of old Jim.

He sat back at his desk and thought about calling Chub. See what that fat bastard would say about O'Malley saying he'd seen him out by the snowman. Probably shit his pants. He chuckled. It was nice to have something to hold over that porker's head. No, better to wait just a little longer and see which way the wind blows. Who knows, maybe there was more in it for him. Could be Chub was up to his eyeballs in this thing. He nodded. Just give him a little more rope and he'd hang himself, for sure.

O'Malley opened the drawer and reached for the bottle.

●●●●

Grant Parsons leaned back in his chair on the balcony of his condo in Palm Beach, Florida. He stabbed out another message on his Blackberry to Dexter. Why wasn't he answering? The next batch of diamonds was ready to be delivered and Grant was itching to go trolling for some more. A new widow had just moved into the condo near his and she was a real stunner. He couldn't wait to start romancing her. The chase was almost as good as the end result. Money. He just couldn't get enough.

A PGA club pro playing the mini tours, Grant made plenty of money, but the thrill of what he was doing on the side was like an aphrodisiac. He couldn't help himself. He was having the time of his life.

He stared at the tiny screen, willing a message to appear. Nothing. Maybe he'd better take a trip to Maine and see what was going on with Dexter. That asshole couldn't be trusted. Could've taken off with the stones. Left him in the lurch. What the hell would he tell his partner, Pedro? Sorry, man, no money this week. Grant scratched his chin, the stubble more than a day's growth.

The breeze was turning cooler, the ice in his drink reduced to a few lonely pieces. He got to his feet, picked up his cocktail to refresh it, and opened the glass slider to his spacious living room. Tastefully furnished in soft ocean colors by another one of his conquests, the large room served him well. He loved bringing his women here. They cooed over the soft shades of blues, greens, and beige used on all the sofas, chairs, and pillows. Called him a brilliant decorator. Hah. If they only knew.

He freshened his drink, adding more ice, and settled into a plush sofa. His Blackberry lit up, a call coming through. He ran his finger across the screen to answer.

"Where's my money?" Pedro's voice sounded far away. Grant could hear traffic in the background.

"Haven't heard from Phillips. Not sure what's happening." Grant swirled the ice in his drink.

"What? Think he skipped out on us?"

"I don't know. Gonna find out. I'm going there." Grant sipped from his glass.

"To Maine? When?"

"Soon as I can get a flight. Maybe tonight."

"What about tomorrow's tennis game with the widow? Want me to cancel?"

Grant thought about it a minute, stirring his drink with a finger. "I'll call. Let you know tonight." He touched end on the screen, then went online and booked a flight for Maine leaving the next afternoon. He smiled. Luck was with him. He'd gotten one, due to a last minute cancellation. Still time for that tennis game. *Good approach shot, now all I need to do is sink the birdie putt.*

Chapter Nine

Kent got in the car with Spike and closed the door. He drew the seatbelt over his chest and buckled up.

His friend grinned at him. "See that car over there?" He jerked his head in that direction. "It's some dickhead looking for you. Not too obvious, is he?"

Kent shifted in his seat, squinting through the rear windshield. "Big guy, dark hair?"

Spike nodded. "Came to see me. Said his name's Walleski. Private dick." He laughed. "Wanna have some fun with him?"

Kent rubbed his nose, slouching in the seat. He shook his head. "Let's get the fuck outta here."

"Come on. Don't sweat it. I can lose this loser. Get it?" He laughed again, the sound grating on Kent's nerves. Not waiting for an answer, Spike put the car in gear and floored it, sending the car into a spin.

Kent grabbed the armrest with both hands, holding on for dear life. He swung his head to see if the guy was following them. All he could see was the fogged-up windows of the guy's car. He hung on while Spike regained control of the car and shot out the back way.

"Is he coming?" Spike asked.

"I don't see anything." Kent checked the side mirror. "So far, so good. Where we going? Your place?"

"Nah. First place that turd'll go. Guaranteed." He looked in the rear view mirror at his reflection. "Whatta ya think of the horns? Cool, huh?"

"I guess."

"Hey, what's this thing ya got goin'?" Spike looked over at him.

Kent reached into his pocket and pulled out a small sack. He shook something out into his palm.

Spike glanced over to see a pair of large stones that looked like diamonds. He whistled. "Where the hell'd you get those? They're not real, are they?" The car slid and he struggled to keep control. A neon sign up ahead cast a blue glow over the crust of snow. "We're here." Spike pulled into the parking lot of Pickler's Motel, a run-down building surrounded by towering pine.

"Yeah, they're real. Got 'em from dear old dad." He poured them back into the bag.

"He gave them to you?" Spike pulled up to the front door and shut off the engine, turning to Kent.

He snorted. "Not likely. I took them. He owed me." He stuffed the sack back into his pocket. "What're we doin' here?"

"Gonna lose that dick, remember? You go in and tell the guy Spike's here. I'll drive around back." Kent nodded and got out.

He leaned in the car. "You're comin'?"

"Right behind ya, man." Spike saluted and started the engine. Kent watched the car, tires crunching over the crusty snow. He followed, with his eyes, the glow of the taillights as they disappeared behind the building.

●●●●

"Shit." I slammed the heel of my hand on the steering wheel. They'd gotten away. Spike's car was gone. I started my car and tooled through Dunkin' Donuts parking lot in the off chance they were still there somewhere. No luck.

I sat there a minute, fuming. Should I try to ride around and find them or give up and head back to the Blake place to see if anybody was home? My stomach growled, reminding me I hadn't eaten.

"What the hell. Might as well." I backed into a parking spot and went inside.

"Can I help you?" A skinny girl, hair in a ponytail, looked up and smiled.

"Large coffee and an éclair, please."

"Cream and sugar?"

"Yeah. And a bunch of napkins. Thanks." I took my booty and headed back to my car, where I sat a few minutes, sipping my hot coffee and enjoying the fresh pastry. Wiping the crumbs from my lap, I started the car and steered toward the exit. I got behind a tan SUV, a couple of kids in the back. They made faces at me when their car turned out of the lot. I made a goofy face back. I could see them laughing.

I headed back to the highway, polishing off the rest of my coffee. Might as well see if they had headed back to Spike's place before I gave up and headed home. I glanced at the clock on the dash. 5:48 p.m. Still time. But not much, if I was going to be home to see Martha. The highway was getting slick, and there weren't many cars on the road. I was behind a semi that was sending slush my way. I turned on the wipers, the rhythmic slash flinging the mess away. I was still hungry and wished I'd gotten another éclair and a jumbo coffee. My tongue felt dry. I could use a cigarette.

I took the exit for Andrews Square and went back the way I'd come. I found the street where Spike lived. Damn. The house was in darkness. So much for that idea. Back to square one.

●●●●

Betsy Taylor stared at the headlines, cup of coffee growing cold in her hands. She reread the article in the days-old paper about Cy finding the body by the snowman. The same snowman she'd passed by a few days before on her way to deliver a nine-patch quilt to its new owner. The story said the carrot had been used as the murder weapon. Had it been there when she'd gone by?

Absently, she twirled the cup, coffee sloshing dangerously close to the rim, as she finished reading. The dead man was from Florida. FBI. A description followed, in the hope someone would come forward with more information.

Her thoughts returned to her friend. *What's wrong with Martha? Why was she avoiding me?* Betsy looked up at the clock, shocked to see it was 6:20. Chub was going to kill her. She'd let him sleep too long. She jumped up, banging her knee on the table leg. *That'll be bruised by tomorrow.* She hurried upstairs and opened the door to their bedroom, where Chub sat rubbing the sleep from his eyes.

"Wha' time's it?" He yawned and peered at the glowing numbers on the bedside clock. He threw back the covers and got to his feet.

"I'm sorry, Chub. I lost track of time." Betsy hovered near the door like a frightened doe.

"My supper ready?" He turned on the light, squinting in the brightness.

"No. I'm sorry. I'll make something now." She backed up toward the door.

He stomped across the room and slapped her across the face. "Don't bother. I'm goin' out." He shoved her aside.

Betsy stood there rubbing her swelling cheek. The skin felt hot to the touch and she tasted blood. How would she explain away the marks on her face to the customer who was coming in the morning to pick fabric for another quilt? She shivered, feeling the hot trickle of tears on her burning cheeks. Hearing the slam of the front door, Betsy went to the window of the upstairs front hall. She saw him back the Bronco out of the drive and head toward town. The stars were out, and the glow of moonlight on the snow was like someone had sprinkled glitter all over the surface. Only a few days 'til Christmas, and now she'd look terrible for the Christmas Eve service. She sighed, wincing. She needed some aspirin and a cold pack. It was going to be a long night.

●◐●◐

O'Malley put the key in the lock and turned back to see if anyone was watching. The moon was bright tonight, a real bonus. He could see clearly to let himself into Dexter's house. The door swung open and he sidled in, closing it behind him. All he could hear was the beating of his heart. Its frantic pace had his breath coming in sharp gasps while he shone his flashlight around the room. *Where did that son of a bitch hide those stones?* He rummaged through the drawers in the kitchen, slamming them closed.

He took the stairs two at a time and raced through the first rooms, finding nothing. Clothes littered the floor of the next room, but what he saw on the bed stopped him dead in his tracks. A carrot, in two pieces, lay on the pillow. The inside had been hollowed out, allowing for something to be hidden inside. *The diamonds. Where are they?* O'Malley swore, throwing aside the pillows, ripping the sheets from the mattress. He got down on his knees and peered under the bed, shining the flashlight's beam across the floor. All he could see was a bunch of dust bunnies and some loose change.

"Where did you put them, you motherfucker?" He got to his feet and tore through the room, flinging clothes and sports trophies against the walls. He smashed the mirror over the bureau and watched the glass rain down over the surface. He kicked aside shoes and stomped back and forth, muttering all the while.

"I'm gonna find those diamonds if it takes all night." He whirled and put his fist through the wall.

◆●●◆

I sat there in my car, staring at the house where the Blakes lived. The night was clear and the stars were bright. All was awash in the glow of moonlight. A movement on the street got my attention. A woman appeared, moving smartly down the sidewalk. She went up the stairs of the house I was watching. Finally, something might be going my way. I shut off the engine, got out and locked up. I hurried to catch up to her.

"Excuse me, are you Mrs. Blake?" I started up the stairs.

She turned. Something was in her hand. She held it out toward me. "Don't come any closer. I'll use it." It looked like pepper spray.

I held out my hands. "It's okay. I'm a private investigator. Could I talk to you?" I reached for my wallet. Slowly.

She peered at me. "Do I know you?" She lowered the canister.

"Simone?" I held out my opened wallet toward her. She inched closer to me and took it.

"How do you know my name?" She studied my picture. Her head snapped up, eyes like saucers. "Cy? Is it really you?"

I nodded. "I can't believe it. The girl I lost my heart to. Still in Boston."

"Come in, for heaven's sake. It's freezing out here." She unlocked the door and waved me in.

Chapter Ten

Simone Blake looked at me, and I couldn't take my eyes off her. We sat opposite each other in her simply furnished living room, where she'd brought tea and some delicious homemade cookies. I felt clumsy, balancing a delicate china cup on a tiny saucer while blowing on the steaming beverage. For once, I felt at a loss for words.

What could I say to the woman who stole my heart away back in the seventies at Northeastern? She'd up and left in our third year, no explanation, no forwarding address. Now here she was, not two feet away. I thought my heart would tear from my chest, my breath coming faster. My hand shook, tea spilling into the saucer. Could she read my mind? Did she feel the same way I did? After all this time, she still had the power to take my breath away. Still lovely, just a slight softening around the eyes, hair still dark with a hint of gray. I swallowed.

"What brings you to Boston?" She smiled.

My heart melted. I put my cup down, leaning forward. "I'm looking for a boy. I think he's your son."

She gasped. "Kent?" Her hand trembled, the cup she held clattered in its saucer, spilling tea on her dress. She put her cup on the coffee table and picked up a napkin to dab at the stain. "Why do you want him? What's he done?"

"Maybe nothing. But he was asking questions about Dexter Phillips. You remember Dexter?

She nodded.

"Dexter turned up dead and then your son went missing."

"Dexter's dead? You think Kent did it?"

"Doesn't look good." My mouth started to water. I could use a smoke. "When did he leave?"

"One night last week. No word. No note. I had no idea where he went. Then he called from Gammil's Point and said he was taking care of everything. Told me not to worry. I was beside myself." She started to cry.

"Why would he go to Maine?" I scratched my head. The urge was getting stronger. I could feel beads of sweat gathering at my collar.

She put her head in her hands. "I told him Dexter was his father." She looked up at me, eyes wet with tears.

"Dexter? When? How? He never said a word."

"He didn't know. Not 'til Kent went there. I never would have told him. My son took matters into his own hands." She wiped her eyes.

I rubbed my forehead, still yearning for a cigarette. "Now I get it. The kid had a score to settle. Big time."

"No. He wouldn't kill someone. No-o-o," she moaned, clutching her stomach and rocking in her seat. "Not my Kent."

Grant sent the ball back at the petite blonde, whose backswing was the best he'd ever seen. He licked his lips, remembering the huge diamonds she'd worn around her neck yesterday. While they played, Pedro was in her room, relieving her of them. The fakes his partner would replace them with were so good only an expert could tell them apart. Grant whacked the ball again. He watched Kelly send it soaring over the net. Damn, she was good.

Game over, Grant sauntered over to her. She patted her face with a towel, perspiration causing her hair to curl and frame her pretty face. She smiled at him.

"You're good," he said. He twirled a ringlet of her hair around his finger. "And beautiful, too." He'd hooked her. He imagined the money those rocks were gonna bring.

She blushed. "How about a cold drink, at my place?" She flung the towel over her shoulder and picked up her racket.

"I've got a better idea. How about a Jacuzzi, at mine?" He put his hand in the small of her back, guiding her toward his condo. "I've got champagne chilling."

"Oh, that sounds lovely."

Behind her, Grant was smiling.

●●●●

Martha sat in the living room with just the lights of the Christmas tree on. She stared at the few presents underneath. Sal hadn't gone shopping yet, and there wasn't much time left. She sipped her hot cider and listened to the carols playing on the radio. It was nearly eight and not a word from Cy. She heard the front door open and someone come in.

"Martha? Where are you?" The sound of Sal's boots hitting the floor greeted her.

"In here." She uncurled from the couch and slipped her feet into her clogs. *He'll be hungry.* She sighed. "I'll be right in to make you something."

Sal stuck his head around the door. "That's okay. Had something at the diner with the guys." He came into the room. "What you doin' in the dark?"

"Just enjoying the music and the lights." She sat back down and picked up her cell phone.

"Expecting a call?" He leaned against the doorframe.

"Just Betsy. Girl talk. You know." She slipped the phone into her pocket.

"I'm going to bed. Long day tomorrow. You comin'
up?" He stifled a yawn.

"Not just yet. I'll be up in a bit."

He nodded and left the room.

Martha drew a breath, heartbeat quickening. She
willed the phone to ring. *Come on, Cy. Where are you?*
She got up and shut off the radio. The twinkling lights
seemed to mock her. She drew back the curtain and
stared out at the snow. The sudden buzz in her pocket
startled her. She answered.

"Hello?"

"Martha, I'm sorry. It's me." Betsy's voice sounded
strange.

What's going on? Not another beating. Martha
tensed. "Betsy. You okay?"

"Can you come over? I need you."

"I'll be right there." Martha ended the call and
went to get her coat.

●●●●

Spike sauntered in, brushing the snow from his
leather jacket. He walked over to the front desk, where
Kent was waiting. He saw the key he was holding, the
clerk nowhere in sight.

"Where's Bud?" He grabbed a handful of M&M's
from the dish on the counter. "Junk food. All right."
He tilted his head back and poured them into his
mouth. He helped himself to more. He nodded to Kent.
"Have some."

"Nah." He held up his hand. "Your friend said he'd
see you tomorrow."

"That's cool. Let's have a look at those rocks." His
eyes went to the pocket of Kent's jeans.

"Not here. Let's go to the room." He looked around
furtively.

"Good idea." Spike headed for the stairs, Kent
right behind him.

Room number six was at the end of the hall, opposite a large painting of the ocean that hung on the wall. Kent unlocked the door and Spike pushed past him.

"Not bad. Good place to crash." Spike kicked off his boots and threw himself on the bed. "Cool. Bud got new TVs." He pointed to a large flat-screen on the opposite wall. He picked up the remote from the bedside table, aimed it at the TV, and turned it on.

"What are you doing?" Kent glared at his friend. "You're acting like this is a vacation or something."

"Keep your pants on, buddy. Nobody's gonna find us here. Bud owes me." Spike continued channel-surfing, finally settling on something. He threw down the remote. "Hey, let's see those stones again."

Kent pulled out the pouch and emptied the diamonds onto the bedspread beside Spike. The stones sparkled on the deep blue of the spread. Kent reached out and picked one up. "Whatta ya think these are worth?" He watched Spike roll one around on his palm.

"Shit. No idea. These are primo, though." He hefted them all in his hand. "No doubt about it. The real deal. Where'd your old man get 'em?"

"From a snowman's carrot nose."

Spike burst out laughing. "You shittin' me?"

Kent shook his head. "I saw him get them."

"Must be a drop or something. We should go there and see if somebody comes with some more." Spike sat up and swung his legs off the bed.

"No way. They're looking for me, remember?"

He looked at Kent. "Right. You kill him?"

Kent nodded.

Chapter Eleven

Chub sat at the bar at The Frosty Mug, nursing a cold one. Clay Dickerson sat beside him, dry martini half gone. "Shouldna done it," Chub lamented, taking another pull of his beer.

"What ya say, son?" Clay asked, leaning over to peer at him. "Done what?"

"Could be my fault Dexter's dead." He drained his mug, sliding it over for another.

"What're you saying? Why would it be your fault? You didn't pull the trigger, did ya?" Clay raised his glass to the bartender and took a handful of popcorn from the bowl in front of him.

"I might as well have," Chub said, rubbing his forehead. "I put those shoes and socks in Dexter's house."

"Wha'? You're kidding, right?" Clay stopped munching and turned to Chub.

"Wish I was." The big man scratched his neck and glanced up at the clock above the bar. *Midnight. I should be home.*

"You gotta tell somebody. O'Malley or Cy. Hear tell they're looking for that kid who works at the mini-mart. You know, the one with the long hair. They think he did it. Killed Dexter."

Chub nodded. "I heard about that. Talk about town is, he's Dexter's kid."

Clay frowned, fishing the olive out of his drink. "Think he is?"

"Dunno." Chub shrugged. "Could be. Didn't have much contact with him. You?"

"Me neither. They're sayin' kid shot him with his own gun, too." Clay slurped up his second drink.

The bartender shook his head, making a slicing motion across his neck.

Chub got down from the barstool and shoved a twenty at the bartender, who snatched it up with a grateful nod.

Clay gave the guy the finger and slid from his stool.

The bartender gave him the Italian salute.

"C'mon, Clay, I'll drive ya home." Chub waved him toward the door.

●●●●

"Simone, another body was found. Couple days ago. Young fellow from Florida with the same last name." I went to her and knelt in front of her, cupping her hands in mine. "Sweetheart, you okay?"

Her face had gone white, as if she might faint. "Clifton?" Her voice was barely above a whisper. "Not my sweet boy?" She started to cry, great wracking sobs that shook her slight frame.

I got up and sat beside her, pulling her into my arms.

"He's your son, too?" I couldn't believe it. Too much of a coincidence. I held her, rocking her gently, like a baby. I fumbled in my pocket for a handkerchief and handed it to her. I ran my hand over her hair, liking how it felt. Like silk.

"It's my fault," she wailed. "I sent him to Maine after his brother." She burst into tears again. I held her close, inhaling her perfume, a delicate hint of rose.

"That FBI agent was your son?"

She nodded.

I rubbed her back, and tilting her chin up, looked into her eyes. "I think you'd better come back to Gammil's Point with me."

"Yes," she whispered.

70

●●●●

The plane was full. Grant pushed his sunglasses up, making his way down the aisle to row ten. He had a window seat, thank God, but unfortunately next to a gum-chewing brat of about five. Grant shoved his duffel bag under the seat in front of him and took the pillow proffered by the flight attendant. He gave the kid a nasty look, put the pillow behind his head, and closed his eyes. Maybe the little bugger would go to sleep, or better yet, move to another seat.

The plane started to move down the runway. The Fasten Seatbelt sign was lit, and the flight attendants were making sure everyone was seated and ready for take-off. Grant hated this part the most. He gripped the armrests, shut his eyes and tried to think pleasant thoughts. He felt the rumbling of the massive plane as it picked up speed and finally lifted off. Quickly, it gained altitude and leveled off. A few of the passengers clapped.

"Sir, are you all right?" A warm hand touched his shoulder.

Grant opened his eyes to find one of the attendants peering down at him, concern on her face. "I'm fine now. Not much for flying."

"Relax. You're in good hands. Can I bring you a cold drink?" She smiled at him.

"How about scotch on the rocks?" Grant relaxed his death grip on the armrests and smiled at her.

"Sure. I'll be right back," she said.

Grant looked at the passengers around him and saw that some were already sleeping and others, like himself, were putting down their tray tables, awaiting snacks. He was pleased to see the brat was busy with a Game Boy.

A couple of scotches later, he felt relaxed enough to lean back and close his eyes. The next thing he knew, the same cute flight attendant was gently waking him. They'd landed. Bangor, Maine.

●●●●

Simone threw some things in an overnight bag, and we headed out. The roads were slippery, and the snow that had started earlier was still coming down. I kept a tight grip on the wheel, never taking my eyes from the road in front of us. I felt blinded by the swirling flakes that came at us, obscuring most of the countryside we passed. We were in New Hampshire, with not much farther to go before we reached Maine. That's when my phone started to ring. I leaned over and pulled it from my pocket. "Yeah? Walleski."

"Cy, FBI's sending in people. They're ripshit they weren't told sooner. O'Malley's on the warpath. Heads are gonna roll. Including yours."

"Shit, Tack, they'll be crawling all over the place. No way'll the kid come back now." I scratched my head, dying for a smoke. "I've got Simone with me."

There was silence on the other end of the line.

"Simone. Your Simone?" The connection was breaking up. He said something else, but all I heard was static. It got so bad I had to hang up.

"Cy? What's going on?" Simone asked.

"The feds are coming, like it or not. And I'm in deep shit. Or so it seems." I glanced over at her. "Don't worry. I'll take care of you." I reached over and found her hand. It was freezing. "You're cold. Turn the heater up."

"I'll be okay. Just find my boy, Cy. Find him."

"I will."

●●●●

"Man, you are really freakin' me out." Spike said. He tossed the stones onto the bed and leaned back.

"I need you to fence these for me. And get rid of this." Kent reached around and pulled something from his waistband. He laid it in front of his friend.

"Fuck! What the hell'd you bring that for?" Spike stared at the gun on the bed, recoiling from it like it was a cobra.

"What was I gonna do? I couldn't leave it. It's got my prints on it," Kent said.

"Don't you watch enough TV? The bad guys always clean, then ditch, the gun." He picked it up and brought it to the desk in the corner, laying it down. He went back for the diamonds and put them in the pouch. He handed it to Kent.

"I figured you'd know what to do. That's why I'm here." Kent sat on the edge of the bed, holding the small bag. "I'm fucked, aren't I?"

"Don't sweat it. I'll think of something. Let's get some shut-eye." He nudged Kent with his boot. "Go on. Get to bed." Spike pointed to the other double bed and kicked off his boots. He pulled the covers back and climbed in. Before Kent could turn off the lights, he was asleep.

◆●●◆

The snow was really coming down now. Lucky for him, they weren't still in the air. Grant walked to the car rental desk, where a smiling clerk sent him on his way, keys in hand. The midnight blue sedan was perfect, he decided, stowing his bag in the trunk. It wouldn't be a good idea to tool around in a sports car, drawing attention. He got behind the wheel and spread out the map the woman had given him. He traced a finger along the route she'd highlighted, toward Gammil's Point. It shouldn't be too bad of a drive to get there, he figured. He backed the car from the space and drove out of the rental lot. The snow was really mounting up. Grant shivered and turned on the heater full blast.

"Shit." The air hitting his sneaker-clad feet was ice cold. He turned the heater off. "Better let it warm up," he muttered.

Following the map, he headed south on Route 1A toward Gammil's Point. The going was tough. He had to keep his eyes on the road and his hands clenched on the wheel. The car slid a few times, but for the most part, Grant was able to keep to the road. The windshield wipers beat a steady rhythm against the glass, the snow coming fast and furious. He turned on the radio to check the weather, and cranked up the heat.

More snow was predicted, at least through the night, with the weathermen betting a good two feet would fall before it was over. Grant groaned. Away from home, in the middle of a snowstorm. Great. Just what he needed.

A few brave souls were on the road, but other than himself and those foolish enough to be out in this, he saw no one. He passed a couple of snowplows going in the opposite direction. One thing he could say for this godforsaken place, they kept up with the plowing. The music playing on the radio soothed him, and he tried to relax his death grip on the wheel.

The snow was pretty, he thought, but they could keep it. He'd take the sunny skies of Florida any day. It was where he'd been born and raised.

Up ahead, he saw a sign for Gammil's Point. Finally. Putting on his blinker, he slowly eased the car into the turn. Sliding to the right, he fought to keep the car heading in the right direction. Trying to stay calm, he remembered what he'd heard about driving in the snow. Steer toward the skid. He did and righted the car in time to take the exit ramp.

His heart was beating like a big bass drum. Sweat glistened on his forehead. Grant drove slowly down the exit and took Route 3, like the woman said to. Within minutes he was driving down the main street of Gammil's Point.

Chapter Twelve

Chub let himself in the back door. All was in darkness. Betsy must be in bed. He sat at the kitchen table and thought about the conversation he'd had with Clay, who'd urged him to confess about what he'd done. Chub shook his head, thinking about what O'Malley would do to him. Lock him up, that's for sure. Obstruction of justice or meddling with evidence. Probably both. He got up and pulled a paper towel from the holder, mopping the sweat from his brow.

What should he do? Maybe call Cy. Yeah, Cy'll know what to do. He rummaged in the fridge for something to eat. He never did have dinner. A package of hamburger was looking pretty good. He glanced at his watch. Too late to call. It'd have to wait 'til morning. He took out the meat and fried up a couple of burgers, devouring them with a big glass of milk.

He swiped his beefy hand across his mouth and put his plate to soak. Glancing at the clock, he groaned. Only four hours of sleep. That's all he'd get. He shrugged and went upstairs to bed.

$\bullet\bullet\bullet\bullet$

Betsy heard the back door open. Would Chub be pissed in the morning when Martha came down to breakfast? Martha had begged her friend to stay the night, to wait out the coming storm and shield her from Chub. She was afraid of what he might do when he got home. She heard the sounds of pots and pans and smelled the aroma of cooking meat. He'd found the hamburger she'd bought for the casserole for tomorrow night's dinner. She sighed. She'd have to go to the market in the morning.

When all was silent, she tensed, knowing he'd be coming upstairs. Nothing kept him from their bed. The door opened, and she saw him silhouetted in the doorway. He lumbered in and sat on his side of the bed. Kicking off his boots, he pulled off his shirt and flung it across the room. He stood and removed his pants, then climbed in beside her.

"You awake?" he whispered. She remained silent.

"Guess not." He flopped over on his side. Within minutes, he was snoring.

Betsy moved over to the far edge of the bed. She punched her pillow, trying to get into a comfortable position. She thought about her life with him. She'd been seventeen, a waitress at her parents' diner, when they'd told her about the fellow who'd asked about her. They'd convinced her he'd be good to her even though he was twenty-three years her senior. He was wealthy, having just won the lottery. That was all they'd seen. The money. They just wanted to be rid of her.

What a mistake that turned out to be. Here she was, thirty years old, no children to dote on, and a husband who hit her whenever he felt the need. She wanted babies, but not with him. She wanted out, but where could she go? Would he let her go?

Betsy sighed and turned over. There had to be a way. Tomorrow she'd talk to Martha about it. She'd know what to do.

We pulled into my place about ten. Struggling through the mounting snow in New Hampshire, we'd stopped at a nice restaurant for some dinner, watching the storm gather momentum, the snow coming down faster. I'd urged Simone to finish, wanting to get back on the road before it became impossible to continue, yet surprised to see Maine hadn't gotten as much snow as New Hampshire.

I helped Simone out of the car, grabbed her overnight bag, and guided her up the walk. Once inside, I showed her the guest room and the bathroom next door. She looked like she was about to drop.

"Can I get you anything?" I stood outside the door to her room like an awkward teenager. "A cup of tea, or cocoa?"

She shook her head. "I think I'll go to bed. I don't think I'll sleep, but I need to try."

"Sure." I turned away.

"Cy?"

"Yeah?" I turned back to her. She was standing there, tears in her lovely eyes.

"I don't want to be alone. Stay with me?"

I took her into my arms, gently kissing her, drew her into the room, and closed the door behind us.

Kent woke early, confused. In a strange bed, he couldn't remember where he was, at first. Then it all came back to him. The wild ride to Massachusetts and the even wilder trip to this place. *Will that nosy private eye still be looking for us? Will Spike be able to help me?* He shivered, thinking about the gun. *Why did I bring it? Can Spike take care of that, too?*

He looked over at his sleeping friend. Spike lay on his back, mouth hanging open, snoring softly. *What will we do today? Can he take care of things?* Kent doubted it. The cops were probably crawling all over the place, looking for them. *Can we get away?*

Spike stirred. "Hey, kid, you up already?" He rolled over and sat on the edge of the bed, rubbing his eyes. "I'm starved. You, too?"

Kent nodded.

"Let's see what Bud's got cookin'." He sneezed and swiped at his nose. "Get me a Kleenex, would ya?"

Kent brought over the box and tossed it on the bed. Spike glared at him. "What's with you? Got a bug up your ass?"

"What's up with me?" he snarled. "I killed a guy, and you want to know what's up with me?"

"Hey, I'm gonna help ya, remember?" When I say somethin', I mean it." He punched Kent's arm. "It's gonna be okay. You'll see. Let's go get some breakfast." He got up and pulled on his jeans, looking Kent over. "I see you're all ready. Let's go."

Kent nodded. His shoulders sagged.

●●●●

Connie got out of bed and crossed to the window, peering outside. Another snowy day. How she hated winter. She looked back at the half-empty cocktail on the nightstand. What was she doing? She gripped the phone and listened to the ring.

"Hello?" Simone's voice came across the line.

"I'm glad I caught you, Simone."

"Connie? Why didn't you call me? Tell me about Cliff?" Simone sobbed.

"And tell you over the phone? That would've been cruel." Connie picked up her drink and sipped. "Where are you? I tried your house first."

"Here, in Maine." she whispered.

"What? Where?"

"We got in late last night. I'm at Cy's."

Connie sat up straight. "Cy's house?" Her voice turned cold. "What are you doing, Simone?"

"He came looking for Kent, Connie. Why didn't you call, let me know he was there?"

"Kent? I didn't know, Simone, honestly. I would have." Connie had a death grip on the phone. "You didn't sleep with him, did you?" Her heart was in her throat.

"That's none of your business."

"I think it is. He's mine. I know you're grieving, but to sleep with my man?" Connie could hear the sound of Simone openly weeping now. She heard a door open. Cy's voice. She swirled the ice in her drink and ended the call.

●●●●

The stack of pancakes in front of Kent smelled great. He picked up his fork and cut into them, blueberries oozing out. Swirling the pieces through the maple syrup he'd poured on them, he popped some in his mouth. He'd never tasted anything so good.

"Great, huh?" Spike said, through a mouthful.

Spike's friend, Bud, stood beside their table. Spike looked up. "These are delicious."

Bud nodded toward Kent. "Who's the kid?"

Kent glanced over at him and tensed. Was this guy gonna report him?

"Relax, Bud, he's cool. I got it under control. I need a favor."

Bud glared at Kent. "Involving him? I don't need no prison time. I been clean a year."

"It's okay. Look here." Spike held out the pouch.

Bud took it and looked inside. He whistled. "These real?"

"You bet. Can ya help?" Spike took a swig of orange juice.

Bud scratched his bald head and nodded. "See what I can do. What's my cut?"

"Ten percent." Spike said, holding a warning hand up to Kent.

"Fuck you. Fifty."

"Twenty." Spike countered.

Bud shook his head. "Forty."

"Twenty-five. That's it, Bud. Rock bottom."

"What?" Kent sputtered. "They're mine. Don't I get a say?"

Spike sent him a warning glance.

79

"It's my neck on the line, kid. Take it or leave it," Bud said, looking at Spike.

"Okay. Deal." Spike and Bud shook hands.

●●●●

"Who were you talking to?" I nudged the door wider and set the tray on the nightstand. I saw Simone had been crying.

"Connie."

"What? How'd she get your number? Wait. You two have been in contact all these years? Since college?" I went to the window and looked out at the snow. I turned back, shaking my head. "I don't believe it. Why didn't you tell me?"

"I was going to. I wanted to wait for the right time."

"When was that gonna be? This morning in the throes of passion?"

"I'm sorry, Cy. I thought it was over between you two. You never said anything last night. It seemed so right." She got out of bed and came to me.

"I think I'd better get you a room at Kathy's. Have some breakfast and we'll talk." I turned from her and left the room, stopping at the doorway. "I'll be downstairs."

I felt like a heel. It was just as much my fault as it was hers. Were Connie and I still a couple? I really doubted it. Too many fights were starting to take their toll on me. I just wanted some peace. Not sure I'd find it with Connie. Maybe this was a sign. Simone coming into my life again. Could I trust my heart to her? I'd like to find out.

Chapter Thirteen

Grant woke and squinted at the bedside clock. After ten o'clock. He swung his legs out of bed and went to the bathroom to relieve himself and brush his teeth. *This place isn't half bad,* he decided, finding soap and some disposable razors. He shaved and took a hot shower. The water felt good pounding on his back. Dressing in jeans and a polo shirt, he sat in the room's only chair and picked up a menu from the bedside table for a place called Sal's Breakfast Shack. Everything sounded good.

I'll have to find out where Dexter lives, he thought, noticing that breakfast was only served 'til eleven. He closed up the menu, grabbed the key to the room, and left.

●●●●

Betsy smelled the aroma of fresh bacon cooking and opened her eyes. The sun was streaming in the bedroom windows. Things always seemed better when the sun was shining. She got up and went into the master bath. Chub had been up already. The soft rose-colored bathmat lay on the tile floor where he'd left it. A couple of used towels were strewn across the floor. She frowned. *Things will never change.*

She caught sight of her face in the mirror and gasped. A large bruise extended from under her right eye to her jawline. After a quick shower, she took a few extra minutes to try and conceal her injuries, applying her makeup carefully. She hurried downstairs, relieved to see Martha at the stove, spatula poised over a pan of sizzling bacon.

Martha turned and smiled. "How are you?" She put down the spatula and came over to her friend. She put a finger under Betsy's chin and tilted her face into the light. "That bastard. You can't let this go on, Betsy. Next time could be worse."

"I know," she whispered, watching Martha go back to the stove. "Will you help me?"

"Of course. Throw some things in a bag. You can spend the day with me at the restaurant. Sal will be okay with it."

"I can't. I've got a customer coming this morning. To look over fabrics."

"We're talking about your life, here." Martha flipped slices of bacon onto a paper-towel-covered plate. She looked at her friend.

Betsy read the sympathy in Martha's eyes. She shook her head. "It's Connie Gaglione. You know what a bitch she can be."

Martha nodded. "This is more important. Want me to talk to her?" She slid a plate of bacon and eggs in front of Betsy, handing her a knife and fork.

Betsy shook her head. "No. She paid me already. I can't get out of it." She took a bite of eggs and winced.

"You okay?" Martha brought over two cups of hot tea, passing one to Betsy, looking closely at her friend. "Speaking of Connie, I think Cy should break up with her." She sat down with her cup and took a tentative sip.

Betsy set down her fork and touched her face. "I agree. He deserves better."

"It'll be okay, sweetie. Eat your breakfast. Get rid of the witch and come see me. Okay?"

"Thanks, Martha. You're a real friend."

Martha froze and put down her cup. "I need to tell you something. I saw Chub out at that snowman the night of the murder."

"What?" Betsy's hands shook, spilling tea down the front of her shirt. "Damn it." She blotted the spreading stain with her napkin. "Chub? Why would he be there?"

"That's what I wondered. I hid behind a tree and waited. You're not going to believe what he did."

"What?" Betsy leaned forward on the edge of her chair, tea forgotten.

"He took the shoes and socks."

"Off the dead man? Why would he do that?"

Martha shrugged. "I think he saw me, too." She shivered in spite of the warmth in the kitchen.

"Did you tell Cy or Chief O'Malley?"

"Not yet. I tried to call Cy. No answer, so I left a message. I'm scared, Betsy. What if Chub comes after me? I stayed in my room this morning when I heard him get up. I didn't know what he'd do if he saw me here."

Betsy nodded. "That was smart."

"Should I try Cy again?"

"Definitely. Do it now. Use my phone."

Martha glanced at her watch. "Shit. I'm gonna be late. I'll call from work. Listen, sweetie, don't forget. Come to the restaurant. I mean it." She picked up her purse and apron from the chair and shrugged into her coat. "See you soon." With a wave, she was gone.

"Why'd you do that?" Kent followed Spike back to their room.

Spike turned to face him. "You want the dough, don't ya? That's what it's gonna take to get it." Spike unlocked the door. He gathered up their things.

Kent leaned against the doorframe. "Was he in prison with you?"

"Yeah, we hung together. Watched each other's back, that sort of thing. Why, what of it?"

"Nothing. Just asking." Kent wandered over to his bed, pulled back the covers, and retrieved the gun.

"I can't believe you left that thing here." Spike pulled on his leather jacket.

"What do I do with it?" Kent stood by the door, holding the gun.

"For one thing, stop pointin' it at me."

"Sorry." Kent lowered the weapon.

"We can't leave it here. Bud won't take it. He's doin' us a favor with the stones." Spike scratched his head. "You'll have to take it with you."

"What do you mean *I'll* have to?"

"Hey, you did the deed. You get rid of it. And you need to hide. How about your grandparents' place? Down the Cape?"

"What? You gonna take me there?"

"Nah. You take my car. Bud'll take me to get yours. We'll make sure that nosy guy isn't hangin' around."

"I don't know." Kent shook his head, and tucked the gun behind his back in the waistband of his pants. "Don't you think that guy'll be looking for your car?"

Spike sat on the bed. "Could be. Hey, maybe Bud'll let you take his. Sit tight. I'll go ask." He got up and left the room.

Kent paced back and forth, unease creeping up his spine like a spider. It seemed like forever before Spike arrived with Bud in tow.

"Okay, kid. Here's the keys. Don't fuck it up. I just got it." Bud handed the keys to Kent, a scowl on his face. "It's out back. The red Trans Am."

"You're on your own. I'll call when I got the money," Spike said.

Kent grabbed his jacket and, without another word, left the room.

●●●●

"Can't I just stay here? Please, Cy?" Simone looked at me with those big eyes and I felt my resolve start to crumble.

"I don't know what to do, Simone. What else don't I know?" I sat on the bed, my head in my hands.

She sat beside me, the citrus scent of her perfume invading my senses. When she put her arm around me, it felt good. God help me. Did I still love Connie? How could I, when this gorgeous creature had reentered my life. I'd always loved Simone. For years, I'd wondered why she left. No word. No note. Nothing. Now here she was, flesh and blood. Right beside me. She still loved me, too. I knew it. Yet, why was I hesitating?

"There's something else I didn't tell you." Simone's voice was grave.

I turned to her. Her arm fell away. "Are you going to explain why you left college? Was it something I did?"

She shook her head, that lovely mane of dark hair skimming her shoulders. She took my hand in hers. "Cy, Clifton is yours. That's why I had to leave school."

"Mine?" I leapt up and crossed the room to the window, fists clenched. I felt like someone had just sucker-punched me. "Why didn't you tell me?" I turned back to face her, my heart in my throat.

She stood and came to me, her hand light as a feather on my arm. "What would you have done? Marry me?" she scoffed. "Remember how you always said marriage wasn't for you?"

"But you should have given me the chance. Didn't I deserve that?" I shrugged off her hand, ran my fingers through my hair. "Christ, I need to be alone. Figure some things out."

"What about Connie? She warned me to stay away from you." Simone was pacing, now.

"She said that?" I looked at her back. "What else did she say?"

"She was drinking. I could hear it in her voice." Abruptly, she crumpled to the bed, shoulders slumped.

I shook my head. "This is too much to handle. I don't need this." I shook out a cigarette. Once lit, I blew a stream of smoke toward the ceiling. "It's over between me and Connie. This is the straw that broke the camel's back." I took another deep drag.

"What about us?" Simone glanced up at me.

"I don't know. Give me some time." I smoked on in silence. I watched her leave the room. *I should follow her. Tell her I love her.* I reached up and rubbed my forehead with one hand and finished my smoke alone.

Chapter Fourteen

O'Malley sat at his desk, fingers itching to open the drawer for a nip. The two FBI agents across from him sat stone-faced, waiting. He started to sweat, two large drops trickling down his back. He could feel them racing to meet the elastic of his boxer shorts. He gulped. What could he do to get rid of these guys?

The shorter one placed a hand on O'Malley's desk and leaned forward. "Why didn't you want us involved?"

"I didn't think this was an FBI matter. Not at first." He blinked.

"Bullshit," the other man said, slamming his fist on the desk.

O'Malley jumped. He felt beads of sweat moistening his brow. "Look. This is a small town. We handle things in our own way. I was getting ready to call you guys," he said, trying to pacify them. He gripped the edge of his desk.

The taller one, Johnson, stood up, towering over O'Malley, who shrank in his chair. "We're in this for the long run, now, O'Malley. Lucky for you, Agent Blake was on vacation, or things could have been a lot worse for you." He leaned over and jabbed a finger into O'Malley's gut. "Don't do anything stupid. Got it?"

O'Malley nodded, swallowing hard. He needed that drink.

◆●●◆

Martha pushed a lock of hair behind her ear. Why hadn't Cy called her last night? What was wrong?

"Martha, table three needs coffee." Sal poked his head over the half-wall and frowned at her. "What you doing back there? Countin' pennies? Come on."

"Okay. I'm going." She grabbed the coffeepot and hurried over. Tack and Chub sat deep in conversation. She hesitated, hovering near Chub's elbow. "Coffee?" She held the pot over his cup.

"Sure. Thanks, Martha." He waited for her to fill it, pulled it toward him, and stirred in lots of milk and sugar.

She turned to Tack. He nodded and held up his cup. "How are you, Martha? Ready for Christmas?"

"Almost." She smiled at him, filling his cup.

"Why don't you join us, Martha? Tell Tack what you think you saw the other night. You know, the night Cy found that body." Chub smiled, an evil grin twisting his features.

She backed away from the table.

Tack's eyes seemed to bore right through her. His police intuition was on high alert. "Martha? Do you know something? Maybe it's important."

She shook her head. "Chub's playing games with you. I gotta go." She turned and hurried off.

◆●●◆

Grant walked into Sal's Breakfast Shack. All heads turned his way. Conversations ceased. He turned around to see what they were staring at, and realized it was him. Uncomfortable, he found an empty table and sat down. A washed-out blonde scurried over, handing him a menu. Before he could look back up, she'd disappeared. Two men at the table next to his were openly staring at him.

He put on his best smile. "Is it my tan?"

The fat guy guffawed. The swarthy one rose and came to Grant's table. He held out his hand. "Tarik Dakari. My friends call me Tack."

Grant got up and shook his hand.

"Name's Chub," the fat man said, struggling to his feet. He wiped his big paw on his pants and held it out.

Grant tried not to show his distaste, shaking the man's hand. Just as he suspected, it was damp. He longed to pull out his handkerchief and wipe away his disgust. He smiled. The name suited the slob.

"Why don't you join us?" the one named Tack offered.

Fatso nodded his big head.

"I don't want to intrude . . ." Grant began.

"Not at all. We'd like you to, right Chub?" Tack turned to his tablemate.

"Sure. Okay with me."

Grant picked up his menu and reluctantly joined them. "What's good here?" he asked, turning to Tack.

"Blueberry pancakes. Nothin' better," Chub said, leaning back in his seat.

"He's right," Tack agreed. "You should try them."

"Sounds good. Where'd that waitress go?" Grant tried to see around the big man.

"Martha takes her sweet time. She'll be back," Chub said.

"Just passing through?" Tack turned to face Grant.

"I'm looking up an old friend. Dexter Phillips. Know him?" The people around them grew silent. Grant felt their eyes on him. Chub and Tack were staring at him, too. "What'd I say?"

"You just blundered into a hornet's nest," Tack said, sipping his coffee. "Dexter was killed two days ago."

89

●●●●

Kent glanced at his watch. He should be in Brewster within the hour. Traffic had been slow but steady coming down, but he'd relaxed once he left Boston. He changed the radio station to one he liked, settling back in the seat. The snow had reached the Cape, dirt-spattered piles lining the highway, and by the looks of the sky, more was coming.

It'll be nice to see the grandparents, he thought. The last time he'd been down had been over two years before. Would his mother have called them? He frowned. If so, would they welcome him?

The roads were becoming slick. *Has the temperature dropped?* Kent clenched the wheel, as perspiration broke out on his brow. He'd never liked driving in the snow, and in his present state of mind, it was worse. The sign for Brewster was just ahead. Kent slowed to let a pickup truck pass him.

"Asshole! What an idiot." He shook his head, watching the truck fishtail up ahead. "Serves the fucker right." He chuckled.

Nothing had changed, he noted, slowing down once he entered the center of Brewster. He eased his foot off the gas and gently applied the brake when a small child darted into the road ahead of him. *Little bastard oughta get his ass kicked.*

Crimson Lane was on his right. He took the turn and peered out the window, looking for the familiar weathered Cape where Lorraine and Gilbert Blake, his grandparents, lived. The house was decorated for Christmas, lights draped in the arms of the two small spruce trees that flanked the front door. A sleigh with eight reindeer marched across the side yard; Santa perched in the driver's seat, while a pair of brightly painted elves stood at attention, smiles plastered on their wooden faces.

Kent smiled, drew in a deep breath, and relaxed. Things always seemed better when he was with his grandparents. He steered into the driveway and parked the car, turning off the engine. He sat a moment, taking in the peaceful scene around him. *Why can't my life be like this?* He sighed. Nothing would ever be the same.

●●●●

I'd been pacing my living room for a good hour and had smoked at least half a dozen cigarettes, when my cell started ringing. I fished it out of my pocket and checked the screen. Connie. Shit.

"Hello, Connie."

"Cy, what's going on? Why haven't you answered my calls?"

"It's over, Connie."

"What? Cy, you don't mean that. It's that witch, Simone, isn't it? She's got you thinking with your little head."

I groaned. "No, Connie. I've had it. You and me, we haven't been good for a long time. And you know it."

"You're an asshole like all the rest. Fuck you, Cy."

The dial tone that greeted my ear was a welcome relief. I shook my head and pocketed my phone. Could I now hope for some peace? No such luck. I heard soft footsteps in the hall then Simone poked her head around the corner.

"I couldn't help but hear. I'm sorry, Cy. I've brought you nothing but trouble." She came to me and touched my sleeve.

"It's not your fault. It's been coming for a long time." I dropped into a chair, rubbing my forehead.

"Where do we go from here?" She rounded my chair, placing a hand on my shoulder.

I shook my head. "I'm not sure. But we've got to find Kent before O'Malley and the FBI get to him. See if he had anything to do with Dexter's murder."

Her grip tightened.

91

"You really think he could have done it?" There was fear in her voice.

"It's sure looking that way. Otherwise, why would he run?"

She shrugged. "I don't know. He could be scared. After all, his brother was just killed." Tears glistened in her eyes.

I closed my eyes, thinking of my dead son. The one I'd never get to know. "Do you know where he might go?" I asked, swallowing the lump in my throat. My eyes burned, yet I was dying for another smoke. I pulled out my pack of cigarettes and shook one out. "Do you mind?" I sat poised, lighter in hand.

"Not at all," she answered. "Could I?" She held out her hand and I passed her the cigarette I'd just lit. She took a deep drag and handed it back.

"Since when do you smoke?" I cocked my head at her and blew a smoke ring upwards.

"I don't. I didn't." She gave a shaky laugh at my look of confusion. "I'm trying to quit. Doesn't seem to be working, does it?"

"Me, too. Kicking the habit ain't easy." I sat forward and looked her in the eyes. "Seriously, where do you think Kent is?"

"Maybe he's gone to my parents. Down in Brewster." She looked hungrily at my cigarette. I handed it over again and watched her take a puff.

"Cape Cod?" I finished the last of the butt she handed back and ground it out in the ashtray.

"I don't know where else he'd go." She shrugged.

"The last time I saw him, he was with Spike."

The color left her face. "Where was that?" She shifted to the front of her seat. "When?"

"Yesterday. In Boston. I paid Spike a little visit and followed him. Guess who he was meeting." I waited for her to catch up.

"Kent?" Her eyes grew wide.

"Yep. Lost them, though. I went back to Spike's, thinking maybe they went there. No such luck."

"That kid's bad news." Simone hung her head. "I was afraid of this."

"You think this Spike went with Kent? To Brewster?"

"No. Maybe. I don't know," she cried. "I don't know my own son anymore." She closed her eyes, tears running down her cheeks.

"Look," I leaned forward and grasped her arm, "We'll find him. Trust me, okay?"

She opened her eyes and took my hands. "Promise?"

"Scout's honor." I raised my fingers in the Boy Scout salute.

Chapter Fifteen

Grant stared at the two men seated opposite him. *Did I hear right? Dexter dead?* That would explain the unanswered calls.

Chub put down his cup and swiped a beefy hand across his lips. "Yup. Sucker had it comin' to him, too, if you ask me." He belched loudly. "Got himself shot in the head. Out by that snowman."

Grant frowned. "Snowman?"

The big man leaned forward. "Yeah. Somebody gouged out Dexter's eyeball and stuck it in the snowman."

Tack placed a hand on Chub's arm. "Okay Chub. Let it go."

Grant eyed the other man. "You a cop?"

"Actually, I'm a detective," Tack said.

"They haven't caught the killer?" Grant asked.

"We're following up some leads now. How well did you know Dexter?" He sipped his coffee and leaned back

"Not real well. We met at a golf tournament. Struck up a conversation and found we had a lot in common." Grant looked up. The waitress hovered at his elbow.

"Ready to order?" Martha held her pad, pen poised.

"He's gonna have the pancakes, Martha." Chub grinned.

She looked at the handsome stranger. "That right?"

He nodded. "They say they're good." He pointed at his tablemates, watching her scribble down his order and scurry away. "She always that skittish?" he asked, watching her retreating behind.

Chub snorted. "Martha's kinda strange. Jumps at her own shadow."

"Not a bad-looking woman. A little makeup and a dye job could go a long way." Grant's eyes continued to follow her as she turned the corner disappearing from view.

"You say you met Dexter at a golf event? Where? Around here?" Tack pushed his cup aside.

"No. Florida. He said he was on vacation. Wasn't bad, either."

"Dexter played golf?" Chub guffawed. "Wish I'da seen that."

"Know anyone who'd want to kill him?" Tack's eyes bored into his.

"No way. Dexter was okay. Gruff, but likeable. I can't imagine who'd want him dead." Grant saw the waitress coming, plate of pancakes in one hand, coffeepot in the other.

Martha put the plate in front of Grant and smiled. "More coffee?"

"Sure," Chub said, shoving his cup across the table.

"Love it," Grant said, holding out his cup. He watched her face color. *She really is kind of pretty,* he thought.

Martha filled his cup and, scowling at Chub, filled his. "Need anything else, just call."

Grant's eyes never left her legs as she turned and left.

●◆●◆

"Does your mother know you're here?" Lorraine Blake poured more coffee in her grandson's cup and sat down across from him.

Her husband, Gilbert, looked up from his newspaper and scowled. "Leave the boy alone, for heaven's sake. He just got here." He folded the paper and put it beside his plate. "Everything okay, son?" He ran a weathered hand through his hair.

"I need to stay with you guys for a while. I can't go home." Kent watched their faces.

"What's happened?" his grandmother touched his arm, concern etching her brow.

"I went to see Dexter Phillips. In Maine." He felt his grandmother's grip tighten.

"Dexter? Your mother told you about him?"

He nodded. "I had to find out why my father never came to see me. Why he didn't take care of Mom."

"Shoulda left well enough alone, Kent." Gilbert Blake pushed the white hair back from his forehead.

Kent was mortified to feel the splash of tears on his cheeks. "He had to pay, Gramps," He leapt up, knocking his chair to the floor.

"What are you talking about?" Blake eyed his grandson as he, too, rose. "What have you done?"

●●●●

Betsy Taylor stacked the fabric swatches in the plastic tub and sighed. Connie had just left. She wasn't happy with the colors Betsy had picked. Piles of red, green and brown material covered the dining room table and two more containers overflowed with splashes of orange. She shook her head and sank into a chair. *Why did I agree to make a quilt for the woman?*

She looked at her watch, surprised to see it was after two. Martha would be wondering where she was. Betsy got to her feet and, laying her arm alongside the piles of fabrics, swept them into the box below. She put everything back in her workshop and closed the door. She'd deal with that problem later.

The sound of the dual exhausts on Chub's truck pulling into the driveway just added to the way her day was going. Downhill fast. She met him at the kitchen door. He stepped into the kitchen, leaving a trail of snow behind him. He shed his coat and handed it to her.

"Whatcha been doin'?" He scratched his neck, and Betsy got a glimpse of the stained collar on the plaid flannel shirt he wore. He pulled several scratch tickets from his pocket and sat at the table, scratching them with his fingernail. He grunted. "I asked you a question."

"Connie was here. Picking fabrics for a quilt."

"That bitch? Since when does she appreciate your work?"

Betsy shrugged. "I don't know. She's very hard to please."

"I wouldn't do business with her, if I was you. Cy's well rid of her."

"You heard? About them breaking up? Did you see Cy?"

"Nope. Everybody at Sal's was talkin' about it, though. She musta been mad as a hornet." He laughed. "Serves the bitch right. Nobody else is gonna want her, either."

"Did she come into Sal's?"

Chub snorted. "Her? No way. Sal's ain't good enough for the likes of her."

"Was Tack there?"

"Yep. And some new guy came in. Turns out he was a friend of Dexter's."

"Really? Who was it?" Betsy drew up a chair and sat down, eyeing the scrapings from the tickets.

"Grant Parsons. Some kind of a golf freak, from Florida." Chub peered at the numbers on the tickets, gathered up the losers and tossed them in the trash. He turned back to Betsy. "That nosy friend of yours didn't call to tell you about him? She was fallin' all over herself to please him. 'Can I get you some more coffee, sir?'" Chub mimicked, hand poised as if he were holding a coffeepot.

"No. I haven't heard from her today."

"Funny, considerin' you two're thick as thieves. What's for lunch, today?" He walked to the stove and shook the teakettle. "Gonna have a cup of tea. Want one?"

She shook her head. "I thought I'd have lunch at Sal's. There's chicken and some cheese in the fridge. I made an apple pie, too."

"Whatcha goin' there for?" He nodded. "I get it. Can't wait to talk to old blabbermouth about Cy and Connie, huh? And that new guy?" He watched her grab a sponge and wipe away the ticket mess. "Go ahead. I'm gonna take a nap after lunch, anyway."

Betsy watched him pocket the tickets and lumber out of the room. She drew on her coat and took her purse from the peg by the door. The cold took her breath away when she stepped from the house. She got in the Bronco and turned the key, letting it idle for a few minutes to warm up. As soon as the air from the heater blew warm across her feet, she put the car in gear and headed for Sal's.

● ● ● ●

We stopped at Dunkin' Donuts for coffee and got on the highway for Massachusetts. The temperature had dropped and the weathermen had predicted more snow. Great. We drove along in silence for a while and I caught Simone eyeing me every now and then.

"Wouldn't your parents call you if he showed up?" I chanced a quick glance in her direction and saw she was leaning her forehead against the window. Tears marred her pale cheeks, the smudge of a sleepless night under her eyes. Still lovely to me.

She turned at the sound of my voice. "I would think so, but he's probably spun a web of lies for them. He can do no wrong in their eyes." She rubbed at the tears with her knuckle. "What are we going to do, Cy? Storm in there and accuse him of killing his father?" She exhaled deeply.

98

"I don't know. We'll just have to wing it. See what we find when we get there. Don't worry." I patted her knee.

She nodded. "Could I have a cigarette?"

"Thought you'd never ask," I said, chuckling. I pulled the pack from my shirt pocket and shook one free, offering it to her. She took it and reached for the lighter I held out. "Light one for me, too?"

She nodded. "Sure."

I darted a look over and saw her light the first smoke. She inhaled deeply and handed the cigarette to me. "Brings back memories, doesn't it?" I asked, drawing in a lungful and holding it.

"Yes. Remember riding in my daddy's car with the top down and the thunderstorm that soaked the inside when we couldn't get the top back up?"

"Sure do. I caught hell for that. Never got to drive that sweet baby again." I could picture that candy-apple-red Corvette. What a ride.

"Have you thought about us anymore, Cy?"

I nodded. "Sure. Just give me time, okay, doll? Don't push it."

"Okay." She opened her window, flicking ashes from her cigarette.

"How about some lunch?" I spotted a sign advertising the restaurants at the next exit. "I'm starved. You?"

"I'd love a cup of coffee. Maybe a sandwich." She rubbed her eyes. The sign for the exit loomed ahead. We took the turn.

●●●●

Spike shoved the key in the ignition of the old VW bug and cranked over the engine. After a few sputtering coughs, it hiccupped to life. He grimaced. *What a piece of shit.* Gunning it, he drove from the lot and turned toward Bud's place. What the hell were they gonna do if Bud couldn't fence the rocks? He cursed, pulling a package of cigarettes from his shirt pocket. Shaking one free, he stuck it in his mouth and lit up. He inhaled sharply, trapping the smoke deep in his lungs.

Little punk could get me in a shitload of trouble, he thought, exhaling a cloud of smoke. He took another drag, grabbing the wheel with both hands when the car hit a patch of ice and slid sideways, then finally straightened. He felt perspiration dampen his underarms, beads of sweat gather on his brow. With a shaking hand, Spike took another drag from his smoke before tossing it into the night. A flash of color in the rearview mirror caught his eye. Shit. Cops. The flashing lights drew closer as the shriek of a siren pierced the night air. Spike stepped on the gas, urging the old car to go faster. The bastards were gaining on him. He shot another glance in the mirror, shocked to see the cops were right on his tail. Slewing around a sharp corner, he felt the car careen out of control. The guardrail loomed out of the night. Spike threw his arms up to shield his face. He felt the impact. The pain. Then, nothing.

Chapter Sixteen

O'Malley sat in his darkened office, shot glass of whiskey in hand. The sting of the dressing down he'd gotten from the FBI still smarted. He knocked off the shot and poured another. *Bastards. Who do they think they are, marching into my domain and laying claim to my investigation?*

He held up the glass and swirled the amber liquid, watching it slosh from side to side. *And those diamonds. Where are they? Who took them?* Angrily, he gulped the liquor, slamming the glass down. He pushed back his chair and reached into the bottom drawer for his gun. He'd show them. All of them. The fucking Feebies and every last idiot in town. *Nobody messes with Chief Daniel O'Malley. Nobody.*

Martha thought about her earlier conversation with Betsy as she wandered down the aisles of the grocery store, searching for something for dinner. Chub was getting worse and she feared for her friend's safety. *Why doesn't she leave him? Just pack up and get out before it's too late.* It was the money. She nodded to herself, hefting a pork roast and eyeing the price. Putting it back, she chose a smaller one and put it in the cart.

Her pocket started to vibrate, coming alive with the strains of Jingle Bells. She pulled it out.

"Hello?"

"Martha? I did it." Betsy's voice was barely above a whisper.

Martha clasped the phone to her ear, not sure she'd heard right. "What?"

"I left him. I finally did it. I left Chub."

"Where are you?"

"Outside your house. Where are you?"

"At the store. Getting something for supper. Stay right there. I'm coming." She ended the call, left her cart, and ran for the door.

●●●●

Connie sat at the bar of The Frosty Mug and glanced up at her reflection in the huge mirror. A bleary-eyed stranger looked back. *Cy. That bastard,* she thought. *He isn't going to dump me. Not over that bitch.* She beckoned to the bartender, who glanced at her from the other end of the bar. He continued to polish the brass rails of the bar, ignoring her.

"Hello? I need another drink down here." She slammed down a twenty and pulled the dish of peanuts closer. The man seated to her right glanced over, picked up his beer, and moved to the next stool. She frowned. *Screw him.* She took a handful of nuts and put them on her bar napkin.

The bartender finally put down his cloth and came over. "One more, Connie. That's it."

"What are you talking about? I've only had two. Oh, okay. Maybe three." She followed him with her eyes as he pulled another Miller from the cooler and opened it. He put it on a napkin and started to turn away.

"I suppose you've heard, too."

"What?" He turned back to her.

"He left me. Cy. Said it was over. Can you beat that?"

"Well, it's not like you didn't see it coming, Connie." He opened the dishwasher and stacked clean glasses.

"He's not going to get away with it. I'll see to that."
She took a long pull from the beer and plunked it
down. "You bet your ass I will."

●●●●

I put on the blinker and turned onto Crimson
Lane in Brewster, when Simone motioned toward a
side street on our right. A yard ablaze in Christmas
lights, complete with Santa's sleigh and reindeer,
loomed ahead.

"This is it." Simone shifted on the seat, hand on
the door handle, poised for flight.

"Wow. I think Santa would approve." I pulled into
the driveway, right behind a red Trans Am. "Whose
car is that?"

"I don't know." Simone shrugged. "Maybe daddy
got a new one."

"A late-life crisis?" I chuckled. "Could be the old
coot likes tooling around town, smiling at the young
girls."

"Cy. He's not like that." She swatted my arm.
"Maybe they have company."

"Only one way to find out. Let's go." I opened
the car door and got out, stretching my legs. "You
coming?" I stuck my head back in the car. She looked
like a frightened doe.

"I haven't seen them in ages and now here I am
two days before Christmas looking for my missing
son."

"It's okay, honey. If he's here, it's worth bothering
them, don't you think?" I came around to her side of
the car. "Come on. Let's get this over with." I gave her
my hand, and she got out. I closed the door behind
her.

"I hope this hasn't been a wild-goose chase."

"Me, too."

●●●●

Martha drove as fast as she dared on the icy roads. Her heart beat so hard she felt like it would rip from her chest. Her breath came in short gasps and she held the steering wheel in a death grip. Ten minutes. Fifteen. Would she ever get home? It felt like a lifetime ago when Betsy had called her. *Will she still be there? Would Chub have come looking for her, forcing her to go home?* Martha hoped not, steering wildly past a dog in the road. The frightened creature looked up at the car as she careened by him. She let out a breath, reaching for her cell on the passenger seat and keying in Betsy's cell number. It rang five times before someone picked up.

"Hello? Martha? Is that you?"

"Betsy. Thank God. Are you still at the house?"

"Yes. Where are you?"

"Right around the corner. Don't move, okay?"

"I won't. But hurry."

Martha ended the call and concentrated on her driving. Almost there.

●●●●

O'Malley sat in the cruiser parked in Dexter Phillips' driveway, a cup of coffee grown cold in his hand. He stared at the dark house, thinking of the diamonds he'd seen Dexter take from the carrot nose of the snowman out at the old Pike place. Why hadn't he confronted Dexter that night? If he had, he could be somewhere warm right now, sipping a cold drink beside a hot dame.

"Shit!" He lowered the window and flung the coffee into the night. "I'm going in. Those rocks have to be there." He crumpled the cup and tossed it onto the floor, where it joined a dozen others. He got out and withdrew his gun, straightening his arms. The night sky was dotted with stars that looked like glistening diamonds. He could see his breath in the frigid air.

O'Malley started up the walkway toward the house, gun held tightly, arms in front of him. The sound of crunching snow behind him stopped him dead in his tracks. "Who's there?" He whirled, finger on the trigger.

A scruffy-looking cat, its white coat matted with dirt and brambles ran from the path and hid in a nearby clump of bushes. O'Malley could see its eyes glowing from deep within the shrub. His legs trembled from shock, as well as the cold. *Damn. It's only a cat,* he told himself, turning back toward the front door. *It's only a cat.*

●●●●

Kent flicked the curtain back into place and hurried from the room just as the doorbell rang. He passed his grandfather making his way to the front door. Grams was peering at him from the kitchen.

"Stay in the kitchen, Lorraine. You, too, son." Gilbert Blake shuffled to the front door.

Kent hurried past his grandmother and grabbed his coat from the back of the kitchen chair. "I gotta go, Grams," he hissed.

"Kent. Grampa said to wait for him. Don't be foolish." She reached for his arm. "Stay here."

"I can't. I gotta go." He brushed off her hand and opened the kitchen door. He turned back to her. "Don't tell them anything."

●●●●

Spike opened his eyes to find a police officer staring down at him. He turned his head and looked around at the unfamiliar room. His whole body ached and both arms were enclosed in casts. The hospital. That's where he was. He groaned. The pain was terrible.

"Do you remember the accident, son?" The cop moved closer, a pad of paper in one hand and a pen in the other.

Spike shook his head. "Ouch. What accident?"

"You don't remember? You were driving way too fast for the road conditions and lost control of your vehicle."

"I was?" Spike tried to shake the cobwebs from his mind. They seemed to be clinging to his memory.

The cop, whose badge read *Smith,* looked up from scribbling something and stared hard at Spike. "You were driving a stolen car. Don't recall that?"

A fleeting image of a puke-green car flashed through his mind. *Kent. His car,* he remembered. The memories came flooding back like a tidal wave.

"It's not stolen. It belongs to a friend of mine. Kent Blake."

The officer straightened. "A Simone Blake is the registered owner. She reported it stolen this morning."

Spike tried to shift his position. He winced. "That's crazy. She's his mother. Why would she do that?"

The officer tapped his pad. "Maybe because her boy is wanted for murder. Know anything about that?"

Spike shrank back against the pillows. *The Massachusetts cops know about the murder? Of course. All pigs eat from the same trough,* he thought. "No. I don't know where he is, either. I was just picking up his car for him."

"If he doesn't have his car, whose is he driving?" The cop leaned over and placed a hand near Spike's head. "I know you know, son. This is serious shit. Don't dig your hole any deeper than it is." His eyes seemed to bore right through Spike's.

Spike gulped. Maybe it was time to let the cat out of the bag. "He's driving a red Trans Am. Belongs to a buddy of mine."

The big cop nodded. "Okay. Now we're getting somewhere. Where'd this Kent go?" He straightened up, furiously writing. He looked back at Spike. "Well?"

His shoulders drooped. Spike felt like a deflated balloon. *It's over,* he thought. "To the Cape. Brewster.

His grandparents live there. That's all I know." He exhaled and glanced down at his blanket-covered legs. At least they didn't seem to be injured. A dull headache was looming at the edge of his vision. He needed some drugs. Now.

"All right. That's more like it. I'll let you rest for now, but I'll be back. You can be sure of that. I'll get your nurse." Officer Smith turned and left as quietly as he'd come.

Chapter Seventeen

Martha pulled into the driveway, right behind Betsy's Bronco. The first thing she noticed, as she glanced at the picture window of the house, was darkness. Where was Sal? She put the car in gear and shut off the engine. She saw the driver's door of the Bronco open and her friend climb out. Betsy rushed to Martha as she stepped from her car. "Oh, Martha," she hugged her friend tightly. "I'm really scared. Chub hasn't gotten up yet. But when he does . . ."

"It's okay. Come on. We'll go somewhere to talk. Make a plan. I'll call Sal and let him know where I am." She drew her friend toward the car. "Get in." Once they'd buckled up, Martha eased out of the drive and turned toward town.

"Where are we going?" Betsy asked, glancing in the side mirror.

"How about The Frosty Mug? It's a weeknight, so it shouldn't be busy."

"I guess. What if Chub shows up?"

Martha snuck a glance at Betsy but kept driving. "Don't worry. Chub won't try anything in public."

The streets were slippery and dark. Martha fumbled with her cell while keeping her eyes on the road. She flicked a glance at the screen and pressed the key for Sal's phone. It rang several times. No answer. But then a click sounded and Sal's voice was telling the caller to leave their name and number. "Sal, it's me. Betsy's with me. I'll explain later. If Chub calls, don't tell him anything." Martha cut the connection and put the phone in her drink holder.

"Can you trust Sal to not say anything?" Betsy said.

"He won't, Betsy. He thinks Chub's a shit." Martha saw the neon mug sign ahead and breathed a sigh of relief. She drew in alongside a newer car, rental sticker visible in the rear window. Killing the engine, she turned to Betsy. "Come on. We'll figure something out."

◆◆◆◆

Connie let herself into the dark house and headed for the kitchen. Her stomach was growling, and it was getting late. Rummaging around in the near empty fridge, she found some cheese and stale bread. She grabbed the butter and made herself a cheese sandwich. The smell of it sizzling on the griddle made her belly ache, as she got out a mug and tea bag and put the kettle on.

She sat with her hands wrapped around the steaming mug of tea, and stared into space. What to do about that meddlesome Simone. *How can I get rid of her and back into Cy's good graces?*

The smell of burning bread brought her back to the present and she leaped up to scrape the half-burned sandwich from the griddle. Plunking it on a plate, she added some chips and sat down to eat. Connie gazed at the tabletop Christmas tree she'd just brought out yesterday. She reached over and turned it on, the bright multicolored lights instantly lifting her spirits.

Christmas. Was she destined to celebrate it alone this year? She thought about the prospect and shuddered. No way. It wasn't going to happen. She got up, put her dishes in the sink and went down the hall to her bedroom. Once there, she opened the top drawer of her bureau and gazed at what lay within. Lifting it out carefully, she smiled. The gun was heavy in her hands. The years of secret lessons were about to pay off.

●●●●

O'Malley inserted the key in the lock and opened the heavy front door. He glanced back. Satisfied he was alone, he entered the dark house. He closed the door behind him and withdrew a flashlight from his wool coat. He turned it on and shined it on the stairs that rose in front of him. The silence in the house was absolute. It made his skin crawl, sending a shiver up his spine. His footsteps were loud in the empty house as he made his way to the bedroom, where he'd taken out his frustrations the last time he'd been there. Maybe he'd missed something. A clue to what Dexter did with the stones.

He stepped into the room, shining the light around at the devastation that lay within. All the stuff he had thrown around in his frenzied search was where he'd left it. No one had touched anything. Good. The Feebies would probably descend on this place like a swarm of hungry locusts. He had to hurry.

Quickly, but methodically, he searched every inch of the room. Nothing. It was when he turned to go that he spotted the corner of something white haloed in the light of his flashlight. It was wedged in the back of the topmost drawer of the opened dresser. How had he missed it? O'Malley put the light in his left hand and pulled out the paper. It was an envelope. He turned it over in his hand, shining the light across the face of the envelope. It was addressed to Dexter, but it was the return name and address that caught his attention. Grant Parsons. Florida.

Now this was going someplace. *Where have I heard that name before?* He was sure he'd heard it somewhere. And recently. Shoving the envelope deep in his pocket, O'Malley hurried from the room. If he could find this Parsons guy, he'd get some answers from him. Even if he had to use force. He smiled. Jim Beam was calling his name.

◆●●◆

Grant looked up when a blast of cold air from the open door hit his ankles. A pair of women entered and made their way to a table at the rear. One of them was the dishwater-blonde from the restaurant. Interesting. He continued to follow them with his eyes as they sat and gave their order to the waitress. The other woman caught and held his attention. She had long blond hair that fell to her shoulders. He admired her curvaceous figure when she stood to take off her coat and drape it across the back of the chair.

Grant stood and wove his way through the tables until he was standing before them. They looked up, startled expressions on their faces. He smiled. "Martha, isn't it?" he asked, reaching behind him for a chair. "Mind if I join you ladies?"

Martha looked up. "Sorry, but we do. Mind, that is."

The other lady smiled shyly. "Don't be rude, Martha. I'm sorry. It's just not a good time." She looked up at the stranger and blushed.

Grant was instantly charmed. "Could I at least ask your name?" he asked, pointedly ignoring Martha.

"Betsy. Betsy Taylor."

"Now isn't a good time." Martha stood and glared at him.

Grant held up his hands, palms out. "I don't mean any harm. Honest. It's just when I see a pretty face I can't help myself. I'll talk to you another time, okay?" He smiled at Betsy.

"Sure. What's your name, by the way?" Betsy asked.

"Grant Parsons. A stranger in a hostile land, obviously." He looked at Martha's angry face. "Okay, I'm leaving. Enjoy, ladies." He went back to the bar and turned to look their way, waving at Betsy when he caught and held her gaze.

"I wouldn't mess with them, if you know what's good for you."

Grant turned back to find the bartender polishing the rail in front of him. He motioned with his head. "Why? She married or something?"

The bartender nodded. "Oh yeah. To a real bastard. You wouldn't want to tangle with him."

"I can take care of myself."

"Hey, can't say I didn't warn you." He dropped the rag and poured Grant another beer. "Take my advice. Stay away."

Grant watched as the waitress went to the women's table and placed a couple of drinks in front of them. He smiled, imagining himself in bed with Betsy, her blond locks tickling his shoulders. She was worth the chase, and he was just the man to do it.

●●●●

"Mr. Blake? Nice to see you again. Cy Walleski. Remember me?" I held out my ID to the big white-haired man who answered the door.

"Sure. Cy, how are you?" He shook my hand and squinted around me. "Simone? Is that you?"

Simone stepped from behind me and smiled at her father. "Dad, please, can we come in?"

"Is everything all right?" He stepped aside and motioned us in.

"We need to find Kent. Is he here with you?" Simone looked beyond him down the hallway.

We followed him into the living room where Mrs. Blake sat.

"Lorraine, where's the boy?" Gilbert Blake crossed the room and sat beside her, taking her hands in his.

"He's gone, Gil," she said to her husband, turning to stare defiantly at us.

"Where?" Simone looked to me.

"He may have killed a man, Mrs. Blake," I said, putting my hand on Simone's arm.

112

"My sweet boy? Kill someone?" The woman shook her head, snow-white curls never moving. "I don't believe it."

"Lorraine, get the boy."

"I told you, he's gone."

The roar of an engine shattered the ensuing silence. I ran to the front door, flinging it wide in time to see the red Trans Am ram into my car. The driver wrenched the car out of reverse, plowed through the snow, and slithered out onto the road.

"Son of a bitch!" I shouted, my breath puffing into the frosty night air. I ran down the drive, watching the red taillights wink out of sight.

Chapter Eighteen

Bud stood at the counter of the pawnshop, drumming his fingers on the well-polished wood. *When is that bozo coming back with my cash?* The curtain behind the counter parted and the bird-like owner flitted through. Bud stared hungrily at the money the little man held.

"Could only get ya two thousand." He dropped the money on the counter.

"Two thousand! Those rocks gotta be worth more than that." Bud clenched his fists.

The shopkeeper reached under the counter and raised a nasty-looking gun.

"That's it, pal. Leave." He motioned with the weapon.

"Okay. Okay. I'm goin'" Bud grabbed the money, making his way to the door, never taking his eyes from the gun.

●●●●

Chub stormed through the house like an angry bull. Reaching the kitchen, he yanked the curtains aside, peering into the dark. Betsy's Bronco was gone. *Where the hell is she?*

"I'm gonna kill that bitch when I get my hands on her!" He tore the curtains from the wall, rod and all, flinging them to the floor. The keys to his truck lay on the table where he'd left them. Chub grabbed them, threw on his coat, and turned back to stare at the phone that started ringing. He crossed the room, snatching up the receiver.

"Hello?" he gripped the phone, imagining Betsy's neck.

"Chub? That you?" Clay Dickerson's voice whispered across the line.

"Course it's me, you dumb shit. Who the hell else would it be? What do you want? I'm in a hurry."

"You lookin' for Betsy?"

"How'd you know?" Chub's fingers curled tighter.

"Didn't. Just wondered if you knew she was here." Clay coughed into the phone.

"Where's here?" Chub felt the keys digging into his palm.

"Frosty Mug. Girls are knockin' back a few." Clay chuckled. "Didn't know your woman drank."

"She doesn't." Chub roared into the phone, flinging it across the room. "I'll teach that bitch," he screamed. He slammed out the door.

●●●●

I crossed the lawn back to the open door where Simone and Mr. Blake stood. A soft trickle of flakes had started falling, dusting the walkway with white.

"You folks might as well come in." Blake waved us in.

"I've got to make a call. I'll be right there." I nodded toward the door and watched them go inside. I punched in Tack's number. He answered on the first ring.

"Where are you?"

"Brewster. At the Blake's. Kid was here, all right. He's on the run. Driving a red Trans Am. Didn't get a look at the plates. Too dark."

"Shit. I'll call the Mass cops and put out an APB. Think he's heading back here?"

"I don't know. Kid's unpredictable. Could be headed anywhere." I scratched my head. "I'm gonna see if the grandparents know anything. Keep me posted." I snapped the phone shut and pulled the package of cigs from my pocket. I lit up and took a drag, pulling the smoke deep into my lungs. Snowflakes tickled my face as they continued to fall. I looked down, surprised to see the walkway covered in white.

I thought about the wild-goose chase we'd been on. We were no closer to catching Kent than we'd been before. *Will he head back to Maine? Does he have the missing diamonds? Did he kill his brother, my long-lost son, and Dexter?* I was still trying to get my head around the fact that I even had a son, never mind lost him. Finishing my smoke, I ground it out on the pavement. Time to get some answers.

$$\bullet \bullet \bullet \bullet$$

Connie put the gun on the table and picked up the phone. She dialed the familiar number and listened to the soft buzz, counting the number of rings.

"Pick up, you bastard." She held the phone to her ear while she stared at the gun. She heard a click, and the voice on the other end of the line instructed her to leave a number or press one for more options. She figured he wouldn't answer her calls. Connie waited for the beep.

"Cy, I think you at least owe me the decency of telling me it's over, face to face. Call me." She hung up and smiled. Placing the phone on the table, she picked up the gun, cradling it in her hands and running her fingers down the smooth barrel. Connie loaded the weapon and took aim. She imagined the look on Cy's face when she answered the door with a gun aimed at his heart. Wouldn't he be surprised? She couldn't stop laughing.

$$\bullet \bullet \bullet \bullet$$

Kent drove as fast as he dared on the icy roads, the car fishtailing with each sharp turn. *How had Mother and that rent-a-cop found me? Should I go back to Spike's or head back to Maine?* Fat snowflakes started to pelt the windshield, coming faster with each passing minute. Kent saw the sign for 95 North and made up his mind. He put on the blinker and slowed for the ramp.

●●●●

O'Malley jumped in the cruiser and started the engine. He leaned over, cranking the heat to high.

Suddenly the radio crackled to life. "Base to Unit 15. Chief, do you read me?"

O'Malley started, banging his hand on the steering wheel. "Shit!" He reached for the receiver. "Yeah. What's up?"

"Walleski just called. Asked us to keep an eye out for a red Trans Am, Mass license plates. He thinks that Blake kid is headed this way."

"Okay, Smitty. Get on the horn. Let the others know." O'Malley clicked off, leaning back in his seat. Little scum sucker was on the fly. He shoved the car in reverse and backed out to the road, slamming into drive, heading for the station. The envelope would have to wait.

●●●●

Martha leaned in close to Betsy. "Where do you want to go?" She watched as Betsy took a healthy draft of her beer. "You can come to my house . . . but I think it's the first place Chub'll go."

Betsy set down her mug and shook her head. "No. I've got to go where he wouldn't think to look. Maybe the bed and breakfast?" She clasped the mug in both hands, absently swirling the contents.

"It could work." Martha said, eyeing her friend. She looked up to see Pauline Dickerson hurrying their way. She groaned. "Don't look now, we've got company."

Betsy turned. "Oh."

Pauline stopped beside Betsy. "Thought you should know. Chub's on his way. Damn fool husband of mine told him you were here."

"What?" Betsy leaped up, knocking over her chair. "Why'd he do that?"

"Never mind," Martha said, grabbing their coats. "Hurry!"

Betsy paused. "Thanks, Pauline." She reached for her purse, tossing some bills on the table. She raced after Martha.

●●●●

Grant watched the two women run out the door. The older lady who'd approached them, sauntered back and plunked herself down at the white-haired gentleman's side.

He watched as their talk became more animated; she gesturing wildly and he slamming his fist on the bar for emphasis. The bartender meandered their way and stopped to talk to them. Grant couldn't hear what was said, try as he might.

Waving at the elderly man when he looked his way, all he got was a frown in return. The woman smiled and nodded. Fresh drinks were placed in front of them. They appeared pacified, raising their glasses in a toast.

Grant motioned to the bartender. "I'd like another." He watched as the man pulled a frosty mug from the freezer and filled it from the tap.

He placed it in front of Grant on a fresh coaster. "Lots going on today," he said, wiping the shiny surface of the bar with a rag. "I'm telling you, don't get involved." He put cleanser on the rag and continued polishing.

"How can I help it?" Grant said, reaching for some peanuts. "That Betsy's a gorgeous woman."

The bartender straightened. He looked straight into Grant's eyes. "Chub's gonna be here any minute. You'll see what I mean."

He'd no sooner gotten the words out of his mouth when the door slammed back against the wall. Chub entered and banged the door shut behind him. The bartender disappeared. Grant watched the big man lumber into the room, heading his way.

Chapter Nineteen

Spike looked down at his useless arms and sighed. *What the hell am I going to do? Where is Kent? Did Bud get the money?* He maneuvered the remote with his fingers and turned on the TV. A picture of Kent flashed onto the screen, followed by one of him. He turned up the volume and listened to the story. They were now searching for Kent in the missing Trans Am, saying that he was headed back to Maine. *Would he be that stupid?* Spike jabbed the button and turned off the TV. Somehow, he needed to get out of there.

●●●●

I mounted the steps and knocked at the door. The snow was really starting to come down now, quickly filling in the tracks we'd made. Mr. Blake answered the door, stepping aside to let me pass. I could see Simone sitting on the edge of a chair, anxiously twisting the strap of her purse. Lorraine Blake sat opposite her and rose when I came in.

"Sorry to keep you folks waiting. I had to call and let them know Kent was on the move again." I stepped over to Simone and placed my hand on her shoulder, giving it a reassuring squeeze.

"What's going to happen to him, Mr. Walleski?" Lorraine Blake sat back down and pulled a tissue from her sleeve, dabbing at her watering eyes.

"We've got to find him first. Ask him some questions. Did he tell you folks anything?" I asked.

Mr. Blake advanced into the room, walking to a leather humidor. He took a pipe from his pocket and stuffed it with tobacco, touching a match to it. He sucked in and puffed, gathering his thoughts before he answered. "Told us he'd killed his father." He turned to scowl at me. "Naturally, we didn't believe him. Boy always did have a vivid imagination."

"It's no story. Dexter Phillips is dead and Kent's our prime suspect." I looked down at Simone. Her large eyes were luminous with unshed tears.

Lorraine Blake gasped, bursting into loud racking sobs. Blake went to his wife, patting her shoulder awkwardly.

"I'm sorry, Mrs. Blake, Mr. Blake. I've got to go. I'll watch out for Kent. And you," I said, helping Simone to her feet, "can't come with me. I want you to stay here with your folks in case he comes back." I turned her toward me. "Police business. Could get dangerous."

"What? He's my son! I'm going." She folded her arms, glaring at me.

I shook my head. "It's not a good idea."

"I said, I'm going. You have to take me. You might need me."

"All right." I was sick of arguing. "Let's go."

"Keep us informed." Blake said, removing the pipe from his mouth. "He and his mother are all we've got." His lower lip trembled; his eyes filled. "Take care."

"Will do." Simone hugged her parents. I helped her with her coat, then turned back to them. "Don't worry. I'll call."

Lorraine Blake stood and went into her husband's arms. When I looked back at them, just before closing the door, I saw him kiss her gently.

●●●●

O'Malley stormed into his office and stopped short. The same two FBI agents were sitting there, waiting for him. The short one gestured toward the chair behind O'Malley's desk.

"Sit, sheriff. Take a load off."

"What's going on here?" O'Malley stomped to his chair and sat. "What do you two want?" He eyed them, thinking of old Jim in the bottom drawer. His mouth began to water.

"We know where you went. Find anything interesting?" the other agent asked, leaning forward in his chair.

"What are you two clowns talking about?" O'Malley said, sweat popping out on his brow.

"We know you were out at the Phillips place. Johnson here followed you." The agent nodded toward the tall man seated beside him.

"Yeah. So what. I think I lost my watch there. Went looking for it." O'Malley felt the sweat gather under his collar.

"If you found anything, you need to tell us." Johnson said, folding his arms across his chest.

"I don't have to tell you squat." O'Malley pushed back from his chair and stood. "Get the hell out of my office." He pointed toward the door.

The agents stood.

"Oh, we're going. But we'll be back. You can bet on it." Alden said.

Once they were gone, O'Malley dropped back into his chair and swiped a hand across his face. He needed that drink. Reaching down, he pulled open the drawer and took out the bottle. He poured himself a hefty shot and downed it. Pouring another, he sat back and shot that one home, too.

$$\bullet\bullet\bullet\bullet$$

Chub crossed the room, stopping beside the Dickersons. "I thought you said the bitch was here."

Clay shifted his gaze from the bowl of peanuts he'd been hoarding from his wife, up to Chub. "Was. Just missed her." He crunched a handful of nuts.

Pauline looked up from her drink. "She'll be home soon, Chub. Let her calm down."

"Mind your own business, Pauline," Chub snarled.

Clay snapped to attention. "That's no way to talk to my wife!" He stood. Chub towered over him.

"Have another drink, Clay, and tell your woman to shut her trap." Chub scowled down at Clay and shoved the little man back down.

"Hey, take it outside!" the bartender said, striding over to them. He glared at Chub.

"No problems here." Chub held up his hands. "I was just going."

"Go cool off, Chub. Things'll look better in the morning." The bartender refilled the peanut bowl.

"Yeah, sure." Chub turned and walked out.

●●●●

Grant watched the scene unfold before him. *That big brute is the pretty blonde's husband?* He was stunned. *What would a gorgeous woman like her want with a clod like him?* He needed to know more. When the oaf left, he moved down a few stools 'til he was beside the older couple.

"Big bully." He nodded toward the door.

Clay swiveled his head in Grant's direction. "Who're you?" He took a sip of his drink.

"Grant Parsons. Nice to meet you." He held out his hand.

The other man shook it. "Clay Dickerson. This here's my wife, Pauline." He motioned to the woman beside him, who was staring at Grant.

Grant nodded to her. "Nice to meet you folks."

"You're new here." Clay shoved the peanut bowl toward Pauline.

"Just passing through, really. Wanted to look up an old friend. Dexter Phillips. Know him?"

The Dickersons exchanged glances. "Sure. We knew him. Was a cop in town. Somebody killed him."

"So I've heard. Have they caught the guy?"

123

"Not yet. Chief thinks it was a kid from Massachusetts. Kent Blake. They're searching for him."

"Wow. Guess I won't be able to get the stuff I came for." Grant shook his head.

"Maybe Chief O'Malley can help you." Pauline offered, lifting some peanuts to her mouth.

"Maybe. Hey, could you tell me where he lived? I'd like to drive by, see the place."

"We can do better than that." Clay said, standing. "We'll take you there."

●●●●

Mrs. Shepherd, owner of Gammil's Point Bed & Breakfast, patted Betsy's hand. "Don't you worry, dear. We won't let him find you." She smiled at the two women before her. Martha and Betsy looked downright frozen. "How about a nice cup of hot cocoa?"

"I've got to get going, Mrs. Shepherd, but thanks anyway." Martha buttoned her coat, watching her friend. "It'll be okay, Bets. You'll see. Get a good night's sleep." She kissed Betsy and headed to the door. She turned. "Take good care of her."

"I will. Don't worry." Mrs. Shepherd waved as Martha let herself out. "Why don't I take you to your room first, then we'll see about that chocolate?" She led Betsy to the stairs. "I'm going to put you upstairs. You'll be safe there."

Betsy followed the woman as she led the way. The room was pleasant and smelled of roses. She put her overnight bag on the bed and turned to her hostess. "Would you mind if I just went to bed?"

"Of course not, dear. Sweet dreams." She patted Betsy's cheek and slipped from the room, closing the door behind her.

Betsy undressed and climbed into bed. She drew the covers up to her chin, shivering in the slight chill of the room. The sudden slam of a door made her bolt upright. *Was that here? Was it Chub?*

Chapter Twenty

Sal drove Betsy's Bronco into the garage and pulled down the door. Martha stood in the cold night air, watching. She looked into the windows, satisfied that Betsy's car couldn't be seen from the street. Sal came around from the back and gestured for her to come in. Together, they went into the warm house, shedding their coats and gloves.

"Thanks so much for understanding, honey." Martha poured water into the teakettle. "Betsy just can't go back with Chub. This is it."

"I agree. He's out of control. I've never seen him this bad." He shook his head, taking down two mugs and putting tea bags into them.

"Have you seen Cy today? Or Connie?" Martha put the sugar bowl on the table.

"Nope. Tack came in this afternoon. He hadn't heard from Cy yet."

"I'm worried about that boy. Kent. Do you think he's still around here? Everybody's saying he killed Dexter." Martha sat down and looked at Sal. He brought the steaming kettle over and filled their cups.

"He's long gone. Why would anybody stick around after they killed someone?"

Martha shrugged. "I guess. Still, everybody's talking about it. It gives me the creeps." She shivered and wrapped her arms around herself.

"Don't worry. He won't come here. Besides, why would he?" Sal reached over and gave her arm a squeeze. He watched his wife dunk the teabag in her mug. Over and over.

"I know. I'm just being paranoid." She smiled at him. Then the phone rang.

●●●●

The snow continued to fall, fat flakes landing on the windshield, obscuring my vision. I switched on the wipers, their rhythmic dance clearing a path in time for me to see the sign for 95 North. Simone was silent beside me, hands clenched in her lap. I reached over and turned up the heat.

"Warm enough?" I snuck a glance at her as I eased the car onto the ramp for the highway.

She nodded. "I'm fine."

"It'll be okay." I patted her hands. "We'll find him." In the silence I could hear the tick of snow hitting the car.

"Cy?" She turned toward me. "What's really going to happen to him?"

I changed the setting of the wipers, the steady beat becoming more insistent, clearing the glass. I looked over at her. "We have to find him first." I checked the rearview mirror. The road behind us was nothing but a swirl of white. "We'll deal with it."

"I'm scared. He's all I've got, now."

"You've got me."

"You know what I mean. I lost one son. I can't lose the other." She sobbed into a tissue she held.

I reached over and patted her shoulder. "Tell me about Clifton."

She raised her head, trying to stanch the flow of tears. "You would have been proud of him, Cy. He was special. Never hurt a fly. Kind to everyone and a big help when I had Kent. You should have seen him." She swiveled on the seat to stare at me. "He'd pick up diapers, powder, anything I needed for the baby. He didn't have a jealous bone in his body. He adored Kent. Little Bro. That's what he called him." She choked back a sob. "He was my life. They both are."

127

"He looked like me, didn't he?"

She nodded. "Whenever I looked at him, I saw you. It's why I loved him so much. I had a part of you. A part you couldn't take away." She started to cry once more.

"I'm sorry, honey. I wish I could turn back time. Give him back to you. Get to know him. Spend time as a family."

I licked my lips. I was thirsty. And suddenly bone-tired. "Why don't we stop for a coffee?"

"Sounds good. It's been a long day."

"That's for sure. And it isn't over yet."

●●●●

Bud Kelly stomped into the apartment over his lodge, Pickler's Inn. He kicked aside a stray sneaker. "Motherfucker. A lousy two thousand!" He marched into the kitchen, leaving a trail of snow. He flicked on the light. "That's it, pal," he mimicked. "I shoulda popped the bastard. Taken all the money."

He rummaged in the fridge until he came out holding a gun. "We'll see who's your pal now."

●●●●

Connie pulled aside the curtain and peered outside. The snow was falling faster, coating everything with a thick layer of white. The weatherman had said it was the most snow the region had seen in years. A record. She believed it.

Turning back to the TV, she watched the latest news bulletin. Two photos appeared on the screen. The first was a familiar face. Kent. That bitch's son. The second one showed a heavily tattooed man with what looked like horns on his head. She shuddered. Ugly thing, that one.

She aimed the remote and turned up the sound. All she got was the tail end of the story with Cy and that bitch Simone being mentioned. Connie flung the remote as far as she could. She stepped to the coffee table and retrieved the gun. "They won't be the happy couple for long. Oh no. Not long at all."

●●●●

Sal picked up the phone. "Hello?"

"Sal. Is Betsy with Martha?" Chub's speech was slurred.

"Do you know what time it is, Chub?" Sal grimaced at Martha.

She returned his look, shaking her head.

"I don't give a shit what time it is!" Chub bellowed over the phone.

His voice rang through the air. Martha cringed.

"Look, Chub, she isn't here. Where are you?"

"Out lookin' for her. Where the hell else would I be?"

"You better get off the roads. Sounds like you've been drinking."

"Damn straight I been drinkin'. I'm not goin' home 'til I find that bitch. And when I do . . . there'll be hell to pay!"

●●●●

Clay drove slowly, peering through the snow that continued to fall. His headlights cut a swath through the swirling white. He turned to the young man beside him, noting his hand clinging to the armrest.

"Almost there, young fella. You okay?"

"Sure. Never better." Grant shifted in his seat, laying his arm across the back to check on Mrs. Dickerson.

She smiled at him. "I'm fine back here, really."

"Hey, there's that snowman where they found the first body," Clay said, pointing out the window. He slowed down and pulled to the side of the road. "Did ya hear about that one, son?"

Grant looked to where the older man was pointing. A snowman sat in the middle of a field where a dilapidated house was set back from the street. "Another body?"

"Yep. Some young FBI guy. Folks are saying he was investigating stolen diamonds."

"Really?" Grant's heart leapt into his throat. *The diamonds? Someone is onto us?*

"Yeah. And get this, people are saying he was Cy Walleski's son."

"Isn't he that private investigator?"

"Sure is. Good guy, too. Heart of gold." Clay checked his mirror and inched back onto the road.

"Looks like this isn't the sleepy little town I thought it was." Grant shook his head.

"Dexter's house isn't far from here," Pauline spoke up from the back. "Just down this here street." She gestured at a sign that suddenly loomed out of the blinding snow. Windswept Lane.

Clay eased into the turn and guided the car down the slick white roadway.

Grant noted the few houses that lined the side street, leaning forward when Clay pulled over in front of a dingy-looking Cape.

"This is it. Dexter Phillip's place. Looks kinda lonely, doesn't it, Pauline?"

"Wonder if he's got any kin?" she said, leaning her forehead against the glass.

"Didn't ya hear? They say that kid from Clover's, Kent something, is his kid. The one they're lookin' for." Clay turned to look at his wife.

"The one everybody's sayin' killed him?" she asked.

"One and the same." Clay nodded.

Grant cleared his throat. "Think I've put you folks out enough. Would you mind dropping me back at the bar?" He squinted through the window at the house number, 149, and committed it to memory. He'd be back.

●●●●

Simone and I sat across from each other, sipping coffee and enjoying a couple of doughnuts. I looked out the window at the mounting snow and frowned. A brace of snowplows rumbled by, their headlights illuminating the billowing clouds of white. Driving was going to start getting rough and I itched to get back on the road.

"Are you okay?" Simone's soft voice cut through my worrisome thoughts.

"Yeah. Just thinking we ought to get going. It's really looking wild out there." I motioned out at the weather.

My phone vibrated on the table, dancing to the strains of "Silent Night." I picked it up.

"Walleski."

"Cy. That Trans Am's been spotted. He's almost in Maine. Just shy of the line." Tack's voice crackled across the static.

"Thanks. Anybody on his tail?"

"Roads are getting bad. Couple of units are down, but we're on it. You . . .?"

The connection was breaking up and I didn't hear the rest of what Tack said before the line went dead. I stood. "Come on, Sweetie, time to hit the road." I pocketed my phone.

●●●●

Chub's truck fishtailed down Main Street. He slowed for a plow that was headed his way. *Where could that bitch have gone?* He gave the plow a wide berth and continued down the street, looking every which way for her Bronco. Nothing. On a hunch, he headed to Martha and Sal's. *Bet that son of a bitch was lyin'. She's probably there, hiding in the guest room.* He'd bet on it.

When he turned onto their street, he saw most houses were dark. No wonder. He glanced at the clock on the dash. Almost one in the morning. Slowing down for Sal's, he noted the house was like its neighbors: dark. He pulled the truck to the side of the road and put it in park, scanning the spacious yard for any sign of Betsy's truck.

Chub shook his head and slammed his fist on the dash. "Where the hell is she?" he bellowed into the night air. Lights went on in the house next to Sal's. A figure appeared silhouetted in the opened doorway. Chub put it in drive and slid off into the middle of the road. He eased back on the gas and slithered past the house. Putting down the window, he flipped the guy the bird.

♦●●♦

Kent saw the sign for Maine just ahead, partially obscured by snow. The driving was becoming treacherous. He gripped the wheel, like a drowning man grabbing a life raft. *Is it safe to go back to the bed and breakfast?* Could he grab his stuff and head back home? Not tonight. Nobody was going anywhere tonight. Few cars had passed him on the highway, and numerous plows were dotting the road, flinging sand and salt.

"I've got to pull over somewhere." He saw the neon sign for a motel winking through the gathering storm. Making up his mind, he signaled for the turn. The car slid back and forth as Kent took the exit, easing back on the gas. His heart hammered in his chest, his breath coming in short gasps. He gripped the wheel tighter as if that would keep the car on the road. Regaining control, he turned left at the end of the ramp. The motel was on the other side of the road. Vacancy flashed on and off in red neon. Nothing ever looked so good.

♦●●♦

Connie lay in bed, gun cradled next to her chest. She turned her head and looked out at the snow pelting the window. It was really coming down now. *Will Cy and Simone be back in Gammil's Point yet?* She stretched out her arm and put the gun on the nightstand. She glanced at the clock. Two in the morning. And still she couldn't sleep.

She'd listened to the scanner and heard that Kent was spotted heading back to Maine. *Is Cy in hot pursuit? With that bitch in tow?* She flipped onto her other side and pulled the covers in tighter. The chill of the room settled over her like a cold blanket. Damn the rising price of oil. She had to lower the thermostat to 62 at night. Connie shivered and listened for the click of the baseboards as the heat finally kicked on. She moved her feet around under the covers, trying to warm them. Her hands were like ice. Would she ever get to sleep?

Finally settling into a comfortable position, Connie snuggled into the blankets, letting her mind wander. She thought of how she'd confront them. Cy and Simone. Then she thought of the surprise when they saw she was serious. Deadly serious. A smile spread to her face. Her eyelids dipped and she felt her body relax. Her breathing deepened and she shifted once again. She closed her eyes and slept.

Chapter Twenty-One

Betsy was drifting off when she heard a door close. *Is it Chub?* Footsteps sounded on the stairs. She bolted upright, blankets clenched to her chest. Her breath caught in her throat when the steps stopped outside her door.

Someone knocked. She jumped, cringing into the covers. Her throat felt like the desert.

"Are you awake?" a voice whispered.

Not Chub. The man from the bar? Is it him?

"Who is it?" she called, holding her breath.

"Grant Parsons. We met at The Frosty Mug. Are you okay?"

Betsy got out of bed, thrusting her arms into her robe. She crept to the door, opening it a crack, peeking out. The handsome stranger stood there, holding a paper bag, a half smile on his face.

"I thought maybe you could use a friend. If you can't sleep, that is. I've got peanuts." He held up the bag.

She tried to see beyond him. "Are you alone?"

"Just me."

"My husband didn't send you?"

He shook his head.

"How did you find me?" She shifted, clutching her robe.

"Wasn't hard. Heard you gals talking and I snuck a peek at the register downstairs," he admitted. "I like the name. Sally Palmer."

Betsy smiled. "How'd you know I'd be up?"

"I didn't. I was hoping."

"I don't know. If you found me, will Chub?" she asked.

"I don't think so. He came to the bar while I was there. Nobody told him anything." He shifted the bag to his other hand.

She held a fist to her mouth, stifling a cry.

"It's gonna be okay. Trust me. I won't let him hurt you." He inched closer to the door. "There's a nice dining room where we could talk. If you wanted." He looked at her, eyebrows raised.

"It's late, Mr. Parsons."

"Grant. Call me Grant." When she hesitated, he took the opening. "Come on. They tell me I'm a pretty good listener. And we can't let these peanuts go to waste." He held the bag up.

Betsy giggled, closed the door, and removed the chain, slipping out. She smiled up at him. "Maybe for a few minutes. I could use a cup of tea. And maybe a few peanuts."

He laughed at her. She followed him down the stairs.

●●●●

When we pulled into my driveway, it was after three in the morning. I was bushed. Simone was sleeping, her breath coming in soft whispers. I looked over at her, memorizing the curve of her mouth, the beauty mark on her cheek. She was a beautiful woman, and I was one lucky guy. I touched her shoulder. She jumped.

"We're home, love." I caught a trace of her perfume as she straightened and yawned. "It's Christmas Eve." I got out, looking up at the heavy flakes still falling and bent down to look in at her. "Coming?"

"Not taking me to Mrs. Shepherd's?"

I saw the twinkle in her eye. "Not tonight, my love." I wagged my finger at her. "But . . . if you don't behave . . ."

135

She laughed.

I went around the car and helped her out. We trudged through the snow to the front door. It needed a couple of well-placed kicks before it would open. I'd have to fix that. Mail had piled up in the hall, and a couple of bright envelopes that were stuck in the mail slot fell to the floor.

Simone bent and swept up the pile of letters and fliers. "Where should I put these?"

"Anywhere." I shrugged out of my coat, watching as she neatly stacked the mail on a small table by the door. "You must be exhausted." I took her coat.

She nodded. "What about you? You're the one who's been driving. And through this weather." She shivered.

"Cold? I know how to warm you up." I took her hand. "Follow me."

●●●●

Bud pounded on the door of the pawnshop where he'd been earlier. All was in darkness. "Open up, you prick." He pounded some more. The gun in his hand felt heavy.

A light went on inside and shuffling footsteps approached the door. "Who is it?" a voice called.

"It's important. Business," Bud demanded. He gave an extra kick to the door for good measure. He heard the little man fumbling with the lock.

"Hold on. Don't bust my door down." The door opened an inch. The same shopkeeper peered at him. "Hey . . ."

Before he could say another word, Bud forced his way inside. He held out the gun.

The man stumbled back, falling in his haste when he saw what Bud held. He raised his hands. "What do you want? Money? I got more. Look, don't shoot." He was shaking like a windblown tree.

"Money? Yeah. I'll take all you got, pal." Bud motioned him toward the register. "Hurry it up, *pal.*"

The man flew to the counter and with a frightened look at Bud, eased around it to the cash register. He held his hands high. "Want I should put it in a bag for you?"

Bud moved to the counter and dropped a satchel onto it. "Fill this. And pal, don't do anything funny or I'll blow your brains out." He cocked the gun.

Grabbing the satchel, the little man opened the register with one hand and began stuffing bills into it. "That's all there is." He held the bag out at arm's length.

"I don't think so," Bud said, leveling the gun at him. "The safe. Let's go."

"There is no safe. I'm telling ya . . ."

Bud pulled the trigger.

◆●◦◆

Kent yawned and stretched, pulling himself upright. He glanced out the window to see the sun shining at last. *Finally. Thought it would never stop snowing.* He swung his legs out of bed and padded to the bathroom. After washing his face and running a hand through his hair, he went back in the bedroom and across to the small flat-screen TV. He switched it on to a station where a reporter was interviewing someone. He turned up the volume.

A red-haired woman held a microphone in front of a grizzled old man, who grinned at the camera. "Mr. Eddings, you witnessed the accident yesterday?"

"Yep. It was one of those young hoodlums. Going too fast." He nodded to the female reporter.

"You helped the policemen, who were there in minutes. They were chasing the young man who was driving the car. He was badly hurt and you pulled him free. Is that right?"

The man nodded and gestured behind him. "Happened right over there."

The woman smiled, swinging back toward the cameraman. "Yesterday, this was the scene of a near-fatal accident. Dorchester police were hot on the trail of suspected car thief, Spike Hanson, when Hanson lost control of the Volkswagen he was driving. It was the young man's lucky day when Mr. Preston Eddings happened to be in the right place at the right time. Sources say that Hanson will make a complete recovery. Thank you, Mr. Eddings." She swiveled and smiled his way, turning back to the camera. "This is Stephanie Lyons reporting to you live from Dorchester, Massachusetts."

"Shit!" Kent spat. "Spike. What the hell!" He aimed the remote and shut off the TV, falling back on the bed. "Now what am I going to do?"

●●●●

Connie showered and dressed, applying her makeup with great care. She wanted to look her best for the big day. Using a curling iron, she tamed her tresses into a becoming style and swept it back with a headband. *Cy loves my hair this way,* she mused, admiring herself in the mirror.

She turned to gaze out the window. The sun shone on the newly fallen snow, glittering like a thousand tiny diamonds scattered across her lawn. It was dazzling.

"Perfect."

Chapter Twenty-Two

"Wake up, sleepyhead," I whispered into Simone's ear. "I'll make you breakfast before I check in with O'Malley."

"What time is it?" she asked, opening one eye.

"Seven." I stretched and got up, gazing down at the lovely woman in my bed.

"Come back here." She reached out toward me. "We don't have to get up yet, do we?" She gave me a seductive smile.

"Well, maybe not yet, but soon," I called from the bathroom. "What did you have in mind, young lady?" I said, mouth full of toothpaste. Not getting an answer, I looked around the corner. She had an impish grin on her face. "What?" I rinsed my mouth then moved to the bed, looking under the covers. She was naked. I raised an eyebrow and jumped back in bed. "You're too tempting, you know that?"

"Why, whatever do you mean?" she purred, as she lifted the blankets. "Ooh, I see what you're talking about." She dropped the covers and raising a leg, slid over onto me.

●●●●

Chub woke with a start. He shivered and sat up. *When did I get into bed? And where is the heat?* His neck was cramped and his stomach felt like shit. Not to mention the sour taste in his mouth. He looked around, shocked to see he was in his truck, parked on the side of the road.

Then it all came back to him. The endless riding around town looking for her car, yelling her name into the night. *Where is my wife? Where the hell is Betsy?*

Bud sat up, shocked to see it was morning. *When did I fall asleep?*

He turned a blurry eye toward the alarm clock and saw it was only seven-thirty. Falling back against the pillows, he reached underneath them and pulled out his cell. *Better call Spike and let him know what's going on.*

He scrolled through his contacts and clicked on Spike's number. After many rings, Spike's voice came on.

"Hey, Spike . . ." Bud began.

The voice interrupted him. "If you need me, tough. I'm not here. Leave a number."

Bud realized it was the machine and cursed. He cut the connection. *Where could that moron be? Probably shut his phone off and he's still sleeping. Wonder how that kid, Kent, made out?*

I'll have something to eat and go to Spike's, he thought, looking at his reflection in the bathroom mirror. He turned his head to look at the sides. Tiny hairs were sprouting up everywhere. Time for a trim. He splashed some water on his face and threw on the clothes from yesterday.

A knock at the downstairs door startled him. *What the hell. Could it be the cops?* He wasn't sticking around to find out. Raising the window, he stepped out onto the fire escape.

"Can I ride in with you today?" Martha asked.

Sal looked up from putting on his work boots. He tied the laces and thrust his arms into a red flannel shirt, buttoning it. "Sure, if you don't mind staying late."

"I'm scared, Sal. Do you think Chub'll be in?"

"Probably. Always is. Why should today be any different?" He stood and shoved his wallet into his back pocket and picked up the keys to his truck.

"What if he tries to get it out of me? Where Betsy is?"

"Don't worry. He won't try anything with me there."

"I think he might." Martha wrung her hands.

"Well, let him. We'll see how he feels when his ass gets thrown in jail. Come on. Stop worrying. Let's go." He put his arm around her and pulled her close.

Grant opened one eye. He pinched himself to make sure he wasn't dreaming. No, he was very much awake. Betsy lay beside him, one arm flung over her head, soft hair falling over her cheek. He'd never seen a woman so lovely.

Last night was like something out of the movies. After they'd had a midnight snack and talked for what seemed like hours, Grant had asked her to his room. He'd been flabbergasted when she'd said yes, and followed him down the hall. He couldn't believe his luck. And she'd been a real tigress in bed.

He lay there just staring at her. *How could she stay with that monster who called himself her husband? How did he land such a beautiful fish?*

Betsy stirred and sat up. She gathered the covers to her naked breasts. "Oh. What have I done?" She looked near to tears.

"Baby, you haven't done anything. Last night was like a dream. And I don't want to wake up." He shifted closer to her.

She threw back the blankets and stood, bending to retrieve her clothes. "I've got to go. To Martha's."

"Won't your husband be looking for you? Isn't that the first place he'll go?"

She sagged, dropping back onto the bed. "You're right. What am I thinking?"

"You could stay here. With me." Grant watched the play of emotions on her face.

She shook her head. "I don't want to drag you into this. It'll be ugly."

"What if I don't care? He doesn't scare me. He's a big blowhard." Grant tried to draw her over to him.

She twisted away. "I've got to go back to my room. Think this through." She finished buttoning her robe and shoved her feet into her slippers. She stood. "I'll talk to you soon." Opening the door, she turned and looked at him. Her eyes shimmered with a haze of tears.

Grant was hooked.

●●●●

Connie dialed the familiar number. She heard the connection go through.

"Hello?"

"Hello, Cy. It's time we settled this. I need to see you. To talk." She heard him groan. "Alright. Come on over. Let's finish this."

Connie pressed end call. She threw on her coat and picked up the gun.

"Heere's Connie," she drawled, aiming at an imaginary target. She laughed as she pocketed the gun and walked out the door.

●●●●

O'Malley looked down at the envelope. *Grant Parsons. Where have I heard that name?* He leaned back in his chair, feet propped on his desk. The office was abuzz with talk of Chub and Betsy. *Good. It keeps everybody busy so I can think.*

He let his mind wander over the events of the last few days. First, Cy Walleski discovered the body of Clifton Blake, an FBI agent from Boston who'd been vacationing in Florida. He'd cut his stay short, flying north to Gammil's Point. *Why?*

Then, Cy found Dexter Phillip's body. Horribly disfigured, eyeball gouged out, replacing a snowman's eye. And the diamonds. Hidden in the hollowed-out carrot nose of the very same snowman. He'd seen Dexter at that snowman. *Does this all tie in? And where the hell are those diamonds?*

O'Malley took a sip of bourbon. *That kid. Kent Blake. He's the one who killed Dexter.* He was sure of it. He thought of the day he'd come in asking all kinds of questions about Dexter. The kid had hightailed it out of Maine, but had been spotted back this way. What the hell was happening to his sleepy little town?

He dropped his feet to the floor and opened the bottom drawer, retrieving the bottle of Jim Beam. He poured a healthy shot and replaced the bottle. The liquid fire felt good sliding down his throat. O'Malley sighed.

Wonder if Cy's gotten anywhere? Maybe he's heard of this Parsons guy. He picked up the phone and dialed.

●●●●

Chub pulled into the parking lot of Sal's and sat there with the engine running. He looked over the cars that were there. No Bronco. He made up his mind, shifted into park, and killed the engine. He got out, pocketing his keys, and slogged through the snow to the door. *Terrible plow job,* he thought, shaking his head.

Inside, the locals were gossiping as usual, the place buzzing with sounds. Cutlery ticked off plates, and women tittered, while men, shoulders hunched, talked loudly with their neighbors. All sounds ceased when he walked in. Women eyed him warily; men looked at him angrily. No one moved.

Chub straightened and walked to the counter. He could feel their eyes boring into his back. *Fuck them. Let 'em stare.* He had as much of a right to be there as anybody. Clay sat at the counter, Pauline beside him. Chub moved their way.

"Clay. Sal back there?" he asked, motioning toward the back.

"Sure. I guess." He picked up his fork and continued eating his waffles. He angled away from Chub.

"Hi, Pauline." Chub nodded at her.

She dropped her gaze, not answering.

"What's going on here?" Chub asked no one in particular. "Did I grow two heads?"

Sal came from the back, stopping abruptly when he saw Chub.

"Sal, how's it goin'?" Chub lowered himself onto a barstool. "Where's that wife of yours?"

"Right here, Chub." Martha came from the kitchen, two plates of steaming food in her hands. "And no. We haven't seen Betsy." She angled past the bar and delivered the food. Her hands shook.

Chub turned on his stool and addressed the crowd. "Which one of you morons knows where my wife is?" Forks dropped. Some folks gasped. All looked his way. No one volunteered anything. He rose. "When I find out who's hiding her, they'll be sorry. Nobody fucks with Chub Taylor!" he snarled.

He walked to the door and turned. "And don't forget it!" He left, slamming the door after him.

●●●●

I heard the knock on the door and went to answer it, Simone right behind me. I turned back to her. "Maybe it's better if you wait in the kitchen. This will only take a minute."

She looked in my eyes. "We're in this together, Cy. Don't forget that. I'm staying. She can't say anything to hurt me. Not anymore."

I nodded. She moved to stand beside me. I opened the door.

"Hello, Cy. Simone. How nice to see you." Connie stood on the step, clutching a fur coat around herself, purse dangling from her arm. "May I come in?"

I stared at the woman I thought I'd known. She was all dolled up, from her perfect hair and makeup to the fur she wore. *What is going on?* "Sure." I stepped aside to let her in.

Connie headed to the living room with Simone and me following. We exchanged puzzled glances.

"What's this . . ." I started.

Connie turned back, a gun in her hand. She waved it at us. "Come in. Join the party," she said, an ugly sneer on her face.

I grabbed Simone's hand and squeezed it.

"Drop her hand, Cy." She motioned with the gun. "I mean it."

I did what she wanted.

"I never thought you'd come back, Simone. Why couldn't you leave well enough alone? We were doing fine until you showed up," Connie said.

"Connie. Think about what you're doing. This won't get you anywhere." Simone said, reaching out to her. "We were friends once. What happened?"

"Friends?" Connie screeched. "Is this what friends do to each other? Steal the man they love? Come back like all is forgiven? Everything's hunky-dory?" She aimed the gun at Simone.

I stepped closer to Connie. "Connie. Don't do this. No one's out to get you. Things just didn't work out between us."

"Stop right there, Cy. Don't come any closer. I know how to use this." She trained the gun on me. "I took lessons. Remember all those Saturday nights when I was busy?" She laughed. "I was busy, all right. Learning how to shoot."

"Give me the gun, Connie." I held out my hand.

"And that precious boy of yours? Clifton? I killed him."

"You?" Simone screamed, "Why, Connie?" Tears ran down her face.

I was stunned. Too shocked to speak. *Connie killed my boy? Took him from me? From us?*

"He would have come between me and Cy. I couldn't believe it when he showed up. Said he was here to help his brother. It was the perfect opportunity to get rid of him. And I did," she said, with something like pride in her voice. She held the gun steady.

A monster stood before us.

"Now, it's your turn." She swung the gun and fired.

"No!" I launched myself at her, but not before she fired again.

Chapter Twenty-Three

Bud got in Spike's car and goosed it, sliding out onto the road. He glanced in the rearview mirror. Nothing. So far, so good. He eased up on the gas pedal and continued driving. *Where the hell is Spike? Why didn't he call back?* He drove down some of the nearby streets, circling back to pull over to the side of the road. It wasn't far from his place, with a bird's-eye view of the front door through the trees.

Two men stood on the doorstep waiting. Their car looked innocent enough. "Shit!" Bud hit his forehead with the palm of his hand. He'd locked the door last night when he got in and hadn't unlocked it for guests. They were probably looking for a room.

Starting the car, he drove back and pulled into his spot behind the inn. The two men had turned to look. Bud let himself in and hurried to the front door, unlocking and opening it.

"We were just about to give up." The tall, sandy-haired man said, stepping inside. His companion followed.

"Sorry, guys. Some folks around here have been robbed lately, so I lock up after midnight." He noticed their lack of luggage. "Here for a room?"

The other man stepped forward, flipping open a badge. "Robert Kelly, you're under arrest."

●●●●

Betsy heard the knock on her door from the bathroom. She pulled the sweatshirt over her head and fluffed her hair, looking at her reflection in the mirror. Her cheeks were flushed and her eyes were clear. For once she felt strong. In control. Chub was going to be a distant memory.

She raised her chin and went to the door. She had a champion now, in Grant. She didn't have to be afraid of Chub anymore. She pulled back the chain and released it, pulling open the door.

Grant stood there, big grin on his face. "Can I come in?"

Betsy stood aside. "Sure." She waved him in.

"How about breakfast?" In his slim jeans and dark blue turtleneck sweater he looked fabulous to her. Like a model with that head of black curls.

Betsy gathered her hair into a ponytail.

"No. Leave it down." Grant pulled out the elastic and shook it loose. "It's beautiful. You're beautiful." He drew her into his arms, nuzzling her neck. "Never believed in love at first sight. But I'm a believer now." He raised his head to stare deep into her eyes, the blue of them like a clear summer sky. He groaned. "Look what you've done to me." He glanced down.

Betsy giggled. "Hold that thought. I'm hungry." She danced out of his arms.

●●●●

Spike struggled to a sitting position and spied his phone on the bedside table. If only he could get to it. He inched over to the side of the bed and moved his cast-covered arm toward it. If he hitched a little more to the side, it might be within reach. It hurt like hell, but he did it. He held the cell in his fingers. Awkwardly moving his other arm, he slowly punched in the number. He held his plastered arm aloft and listened for the ring. The machine picked up. He groaned. Bud's voice came across the line, spouting off how to leave a message. Spike let the phone drop.

●●●●

"What do you think he'll do?" Pauline asked Martha.

Martha paused for a moment then continued filling saltshakers. "I don't know." She shuddered, thinking about what he'd do if he found Betsy. And what he'd do to Sal and her when he found out they'd helped in her escape.

Pauline pushed her cup closer. "Could I trouble you for more coffee, Martha?"

"I'm sorry. Sure, Pauline." Martha put the salt container under the counter and reached for the coffeepot. "Let me make a fresh pot, okay?"

Pauline nodded. "Chub's a loose cannon just waiting to go off."

Sal came from the back. "I heard that. I agree. Something's gonna happen." He put a plate of bacon and eggs on the counter and went around the other side to sit beside Pauline. He leaned over and looked around. "Where'd Clay go?"

"Men's room, I think." Pauline smiled at Martha, who filled her cup.

Martha poured a cup of coffee and came to join them. "Has anybody heard from Cy? Or Connie?"

"Tack talked to Cy. Last I heard, he and that new lady friend of his were on their way back here." Sal sopped up egg with his toast. He turned over his cup. Martha went to fill it.

"I got a bad feelin' about all this," Pauline said, gazing into her coffee.

Clay sidled onto his stool. "What's goin' on? Anybody know where Betsy went?"

Martha and Sal exchanged glances.

"Chub's your friend, Clay. If we knew, you'd be the last person we'd tell." Martha said, sipping her coffee.

"Aw, come on. I won't tell. He's no friend of mine. Not after the way he treated my sweetie," he said, putting his hand on Pauline's.

149

"You sure?" Sal asked.

"Yep. Cross my heart." Clay drew his finger across his chest.

"We took her to Shepherd's," Martha said, looking from Clay to his wife.

Pauline's brows rose. "The bed and breakfast? Won't he look there?"

"Hope not." Sal answered, chewing the last of his bacon.

Martha turned to Sal. "It's slowed down here. Would you mind if I checked on her?"

He shook his head. "Go on. I'll hold down the fort."

"I'm coming with you," Pauline said, standing and slipping her arms into her coat.

"No, stay here. In case she shows up again."

Pauline nodded and took off her coat, sitting back down.

◆◆◆◆

The pain in my foot was horrible, but the pain in my heart was worse. Simone lay on the floor nearby. Connie had dropped the gun and stood, face in her hands, sobbing. I hobbled over and retrieved the gun, making my painful way to Simone.

"Baby?" I sank to my knees. My foot was on fire, my shoe filling with blood. I felt for a pulse. There was none. "No!" I gathered her into my arms. Her beautiful eyes were vacant. I hugged her close, her blood soaking my shirt.

Connie looked down at me, a blank expression on her face.

Gently, I lowered Simone to the floor and pulled out my cell. I dialed. "I'd like to report a murder," I choked out. I gave the street information to the dispatcher and ended the call.

●●●●

"Chief O'Malley, there's been a shooting. At Cy's place." Smitty poked his head into the office.

"What the hell! Get my car. Hurry up." O'Malley stood, reaching in the top drawer for his gun, shot glass of bourbon forgotten. He threw on his coat and put on his gloves, striding for the door.

"All set, Chief." Smitty nodded grimly at him from the opened door.

"Where's Tack?" O'Malley looked around.

"On his way, sir. To the house."

Two officers came from the back room, their expressions serious.

"You, come with me." O'Malley signaled to one. He turned to his people. "The rest of you, monitor the radio and keep me informed of anything else that goes down. Got that?"

The officers nodded.

O'Malley left with the lone officer trailing him.

●●●●

Mrs. Shepherd had laid out a delicious array of foods to choose from. Betsy and Grant helped themselves and sat down to eat. Grant had a blueberry muffin halfway to his mouth when his cell phone rang.

"Yeah?"

"Where the hell are you, man?" Pedro's voice had an edge to it.

"Still in Maine. What's wrong?"

"I heard some guy was nabbed for stolen diamonds up there. Nothing to do with us, is it?"

"Shit! I hope not." Grant looked over at Betsy. Her face was white. She looked about to faint. He held the phone against his chest. "It's okay, don't worry. Just business," he said to her.

"You're not mixed up with some dame, are you?" Pedro asked.

"Don't worry. I'll handle it. I'll get back to you later." He ended the call.

"Is everything all right?" Betsy held her teacup with shaking hands.

"Sure. Finish your breakfast. I've got something I have to do. Stay here." He stood, leaned over her and kissed the top of her head. "I'll be back."

⁘

Bud stared at the two men brandishing FBI badges. They moved swiftly, hustling him out to their car. *How did they find me? And so fast?* He stared out at the passing scenery, wondering if that little twerp, Kent had given him up. *And Spike. Is he okay?*

The agent in the passenger seat swiveled to look at him. "You're in a lot of trouble, Kelly. You'd better sing like a bird when we bring you in."

"You ain't got nothin' on me," he said, pulling at the cuffs that bit into his wrists.

"Oh, we've got plenty, my man. You can bet on it," the driver said, looking at Bud in the rearview mirror.

"Hey, I'm from Massachusetts, not that hick town in Maine! I want a lawyer. I got rights."

"You'll get your lawyer and fifteen minutes of fame. After that, it's back in the slammer for you," the driver said, a smirk on his face.

Bud glared at them. A couple of shitheads. He leaned back. Nothing to do but wait.

Chapter Twenty-Four

Through the haze of pain I was dimly aware of the sound of sirens. I'd removed my shoe and wrapped my blood-soaked sock around my foot, tightening it as much as I could. Connie hovered in the background, wringing her hands. I'd closed my Simone's eyes, kissing her for the last time. I couldn't cry. There was a hollow feeling deep inside my gut. I'd barely found her, only to have her taken from me. This time for good.

A pounding at the door roused me. "In here," I shouted. I heard the sound of many feet coming our way.

"Cy! What happened?" Tack strode over to me, gun held on Connie.

Uniformed policemen suddenly filled the room. Connie was handcuffed and led away, the gun retrieved for evidence.

Tack pointed to Simone's crumpled form when the EMTs rushed in, and I watched them check for signs of life. I already knew what they'd find. She was gone from me forever.

◆●◆●

Kent spent the morning calling hospitals in the Boston area until he found Spike. The receptionist informed him that he wasn't allowed calls. He cut the connection when she asked his name. *What the hell was that all about? Are the cops there?*

He paced the room like a nervous cat. *What should I do? Does Bud have the money, or is he still holding the stones?*

"Calm down," he said to himself, sitting on the bed. "I gotta think." He ran his hands through his hair. "I'll get my stuff at the bed and breakfast and go home. Bud'll call." He grabbed the duffle he'd brought and unzipped it. The gun was still there. He stuffed his things on top of it, zipping it closed.

When he stepped out of the room, the sun nearly blinded him, reflecting off the crust of snow covering everything. He stowed his bag in the Trans Am and brought the key to the office. The sleepy clerk barely acknowledged him.

Taking a final look around, he got in the car and headed back out to the highway.

Chub was just about to pass the bed and breakfast when he saw someone come out the front door. The new guy. Grant Parsons. He slowed, pulled over, and tugged his wool cap down tight. He hunkered down in the seat and watched the man walk to a car in the parking lot and get in. He didn't start the car, just sat there. Was he on a cell phone?

Reaching for the door handle, Chub hesitated. Could his wife be with this jerk? He was gonna find out.

"The Feebies got a guy we've been watching," Tack said, helping me into his car. "A known felon out on parole, Robert Kelly. We found out he and Spike were tight in prison." Tack looked over at me, his mouth a thin line.

"I think Kent got the diamonds and brought them to his buddy to fence." I winced when we went over

154

a bump. My throat was raw, tears hovering at the corners of my eyes.

Tack nodded. "Yep. There was a shooting at a Dorchester pawnshop. The owner took a bullet. Didn't make it. But he lived long enough to ID Kelly."

"Did you recover the stones?" I looked down at my throbbing foot and readjusted it. A sob caught in my throat. *How am I going to go on?*

"Not yet. Working on it, though."

"Look, I'm not staying," I said, as we pulled into the hospital emergency entrance.

"Just get it looked at, okay? Let 'em bandage it up." Tack pulled up to the door, and a guy came out with a wheelchair.

"I can walk." I opened the car door, swinging my legs free.

"Humor me," Tack said, coming around to hold the door.

I nodded. The fellow in white helped me into the chair and took me inside, Tack bringing up the rear.

$$\bullet\!\bullet\!\bullet\!\bullet$$

O'Malley shot a glance at his prisoner. Connie Gaglione sat on the cot, head in her hands. She hadn't uttered a single word since they'd brought her in over an hour ago. *Why'd she do it?* He wondered. *Was she that hooked on Walleski that she'd take a life?* No, make that two lives. On the ride in she'd confessed to killing the FBI agent Cy had found out by that snowman. And now this Blake dame. *Walleski and his women.* O'Malley shook his head.

"Those two agents from the FBI want to talk to you, Chief," Smitty said, sticking his head through the door. "Should I send 'em in?"

"Yeah. Okay." O'Malley put down his feet and grabbed the empty shot glass. He opened the bottom drawer and put in the glass with Old Jim. Just in time. The two hot shots breezed in.

155

"We got someone you might want to speak to, O'Malley. He's been processed." Alden, the sandy-haired agent, took a seat across from O'Malley and hooked his hands behind his head, big smirk on his face.

I'd like to wipe the smile off that little asshole's face, O'Malley thought. He leaned back, hands in his lap. "Yeah? And who's that?"

"Robert Kelly. Friend of Kent Blake. The kid you're looking for." The other agent spoke up from the doorway.

O'Malley looked from one to the other and frowned. "Okay. Bring him in."

"Not so fast. It's time you filled us in on everything," the big guy at the door said. He made no move to sit.

O'Malley sighed. "All right. Let me talk to him. We'll share what we've got so far."

Alden got up and took the glass paperweight from O'Malley's desk. He hefted it in his hand. Looking to his partner, he shifted the globe from hand to hand. "What do you think, Johnson? Do we trust him?"

The tall agent shrugged. "Why don't we find out?"

●●●●

Martha mounted the steps of the Gammil's Point Bed and Breakfast, about to go through the door when something stopped her. She turned and saw Chub's truck idling by the side of the road. She gulped. *What is he doing here?* She scanned the parking lot to see what he could be looking at. The rental car. Grant Parsons was here. *Could he have found Betsy? Is Chub waiting to see if his wife would come out? With Grant?* But, no. She squinted harder. She could see someone in the dark blue sedan.

Martha swiveled to look in Chub's direction. *No!* He was getting out of his truck. Going toward the car. She didn't wait to see what would happen. Martha opened the door and scurried inside.

●●●●

Betsy finished her breakfast and hurried up to her room. Mrs. Shepherd was poised to knock, fresh towels over her arm.

"Hello, Mrs. Shepherd." Betsy walked toward her.

The older woman straightened, turning her way. "Betsy, call me Doris. No need for formality here." She smiled at her.

"I can take those." Betsy reached for the towels.

Doris Shepherd handed them to her. "Did you have enough to eat, dear?"

"It was . . ."

The front door slammed shut. Both women jumped.

"My goodness . . ." Doris Shepherd gasped.

Footsteps sounded on the stairs. Martha appeared. "Betsy, Chub's outside!" Winded, she sat on the top step.

"Chub?" Betsy's breath caught in her throat. "How'd he find me?"

Martha got up. "I don't think he knows you're here. But he saw that new guy in his car. When I came in, he was going over to him."

"Grant?"

Martha nodded. She turned to Doris. "Is there a back door?"

The older woman motioned to them. "Come on, I'll show you."

●●●●

"Where do you think you're going?" Tack put an arm out to stop me.

"I got to find Kent before the FBI does." Reluctantly, I lowered myself into the wheelchair a young nurse was holding onto. I turned back to look at my friend. "You coming?"

Tack nodded. "Stubborn fool. My car's just outside."

157

The little nurse maneuvered me out the emergency room door, with Tack close behind. I could hear him jingling his keys. The going was tricky, ice on the walkways slowing our progress. We stopped to wait for him to catch up.

"Going to a fire?" Tack asked, coming to stand beside me. "Careful. Let's get you inside." He took my free arm and guided me into the car, with the nurse's help. "Can't have you falling."

"I'm okay," I said, grimacing. "I can manage." The image of Simone lying on the floor, dead eyes staring up at me came into my mind. I choked back a sob.

Another nurse appeared carrying a new set of crutches, and stowed them in the back seat, with Tack's help

"You okay, Cy?"

I nodded and gulped. "I need clean clothes." I looked down at my blood-soaked things. My stomach churned at the thought of whose blood it was. Simone. I swallowed the lump in my throat and turned my head. Couldn't let him see my tears.

Tack started the car and drove out of the lot. "For what it's worth? I'm sorry, man." He laid his hand on my arm.

I could feel his eyes on me.

"Let's find that kid." I leaned my head back and closed my eyes.

Chapter Twenty-Five

Chub went up to the car and knocked on the window. "Get out here!"

Grant started and turned to see the big man glaring at him. He clapped his phone shut and got out. "What do you want?"

Chub got in his face. "My wife, for starters. Where is she?" he snarled.

"How should I know? I'm not her keeper." He backed up.

Chub advanced on him. "I think you do know. Folks at Sal's said you were cozyin' up to her. Ain't that right?" He grabbed the front of Grant's coat. "I oughta wring your scrawny little neck."

Grant pulled out of his grasp. "You better leave. I called nine-one-one. Cops should be here any minute." He tensed, wondering if the hulk believed him.

Chub's face contorted. "I'm not done with you yet. I'll be back." He turned and stomped off through the snow to a truck parked at the side of the road.

Grant shivered, drawing his coat tight. He watched as the truck slid around to disappear down the road.

●●●●

"I got nothin' to say to you." Bud slid down in his chair, glaring at the policeman and two FBI agents.

"You little worm! I can squash you in a minute. Where's Kent Blake?" O'Malley kicked at the leg of the chair.

"Come on, Bud. Make it easy on yourself. Let's cut a deal." The taller FBI agent grinned at him from the door.

"I want a lawyer."

"I want a lawyer," O'Malley mimicked, circling Bud's chair. "Tell us where that little twerp is." He leaned down to look in the prisoner's face.

"Look, I can make them go easy on you." Agent Alden leaned against O'Malley's desk, arms folded. "Just tell us."

Bud started to sweat. He could feel the sheriff's hot breath in his face. He smelled liquor. "Take these off." He held out his cuffed hands.

"Sure." O'Malley said, straightening, yanking Bud up by the handcuffs. "Just as soon as you tell us."

Bud spit in his face.

Martha and Betsy peeked out the back door, Doris Shepherd just behind them. They could see the path she pointed out to them through towering evergreens, boughs heavy with snow.

"Will you be okay?" Doris asked, wringing her hands.

Martha turned and put her hand on the older woman's shoulder. "Go back inside. Don't tell anyone we were here, okay?"

Doris nodded. "Hurry. And be careful."

Betsy hugged her. "Thank you. Go in, before you catch cold." She shooed her toward the door, then followed her best friend through the snow.

I made my way, on my crutches, to the front door and pulled at the yellow crime-scene tape. I whipped it aside. No one was keeping me out of my own house. Not even the police. Tack stomped his feet behind me, and we went in.

All was quiet. I could see the outlines they'd made where Simone's body had been. I groaned.

"Come on, Cy. I'll get you some clean stuff." Tack touched my sleeve.

I heard him go upstairs and the banging of drawers. I eased down into my recliner. I couldn't take my eyes from that spot. Where all my hopes and dreams had died. Simone.

I moaned, dropping my head into my hands. The pain of losing her was tearing at my gut like a wild animal.

"Cy?" I felt a hand on my shoulder. "I've got your things." Tack handed me a clean shirt and jeans. "I just got a call. O'Malley's got Robert Kelly. The guy who fenced the diamonds."

My head shot up. "Kelly?" I shrugged out of my shirt and put on the fresh one. Kicking off my one loafer, I stood awkwardly and dropped my pants. I struggled to get the jeans on over my bandaged foot. Tack bent to help me. I looked into his face. "Let's go."

●●●●

Chub drove like a mad man. He flew down streets, swerving and sliding, slush flying from behind the tires. He slammed his fist on the steering wheel. *Martha.* That bitch knew something. He was sure of it. And he was going to get it out of her. Even if he had to kill her. He turned onto Main Street and headed for Sal's.

●●●●

Grant let himself in and hurried up the stairs to Betsy's room. Finding the door ajar, he went inside. "Honey? You in here?" He went to the bathroom door and pushed it open. Empty.

Where is she? Still eating breakfast? He shook his head. She would have heard him come in. Looked for him.

161

Concerned, he headed back downstairs. Mrs. Shepherd stood at the bottom, waiting for him. "What's wrong?" he asked, stepping off the last stair.

She was wringing her hands. "They've gone. She went with Martha."

"Where?" His throat tightened.

"I told them about a trail in the woods all the kids use. Out behind the house. It comes out by Clover's Mini Mart." She shivered.

"Betsy's husband was here. Looking for her," Grant said.

"I know. What did you tell him?"

"Nothing. He's dangerous. Out of control."

"I'm going to call the police." She picked up the phone from the front desk.

Grant pulled a gun from his waistband. "I'm going after them."

●●●●

I limped into the station with Tack. Smitty pointed toward the back. I didn't wait for an invitation.

O'Malley looked up from his desk, a smirk on his face. "Lookee who we got here, Walleski. A pal of Kent's." He nodded toward a bald-headed guy in a chair. He was wearing bracelets, compliments of the police. Across the room stood a couple of strangers. They nodded at me.

"This Robert Kelly?" I asked. The man in cuffs glowered at me. I nodded at the two men. "And these guys are . . .?"

"Special agent Alden," the smaller of the two said, stepping forward to shake my hand.

"That one's Johnson." O'Malley said, jerking his chin in the other guy's direction.

The agent nodded at me.

"Has he given up Kent?" I looked at O'Malley.

His face was flushed and he needed a shave. "Naw. Thinks he can outsmart us. Well, he ain't gonna outrun a murder conviction." He ran a hand through his hair.

"The pawn shop guy?" I hobbled over to O'Malley's desk, turning to face Bud Kelly. "Why'd you kill him?" I asked, looking into his eyes.

"He screwed me," he spat.

"Over the diamonds?" I said.

He nodded, slumping down in his chair. "Yeah. The diamonds."

●●●●

Betsy slithered and slid down the path, hurrying after Martha. "Slow down," she begged, panting.

Martha looked over her shoulder at her friend. Her face was red from the cold and she looked ready to collapse. Martha slowed. "We've got to keep moving. What if Chub comes back?"

Betsy caught up to her. "I know. Just let me catch my breath. It's cold out here." She shivered, wrapping her arms around herself.

"Doris said this path comes out behind Clover's. Maybe we can get someone there to give us a ride to my place." Martha touched Betsy's arm. "Don't worry, I won't leave you."

Betsy flung herself into her friend's arms. "Oh, Martha. I'm scared."

●●●●

Kent pulled into the parking lot of the bed and breakfast and parked next to a dark blue sedan. Only a handful of cars were there and all were covered by a thick coat of snow. Except the sedan. Someone had recently cleared it. Large wet drops shimmered on the windshield in the morning sun. Heat still rose from the engine.

Kicking open the car door, Kent got out and stretched. He scanned the area surrounding the inn. No one around. A sudden movement from the side of the building caught his eye. A figure moved off toward the woods, gun in hand. Kent dropped into a crouch and watched as the person disappeared from view.

What's going on? Who the hell was that? He stayed where he was for a few more minutes before rising and heading for the front door.

● ● ● ●

Martha grabbed Betsy's hand, hauling her farther into the woods. Every sound stopped them in their tracks, chests heaving, eyes furtively checking the trees and dark corners around them. Only a pair of frightened deer stared back at them before leaping into the underbrush, the sound of their escape loud in the silence of the woods.

Martha saw the road ahead through a break in the trees. Clover's familiar sign was off to their left. She halted Betsy with a finger to her lips, and pointed to the welcome sight of the small store.

"Do you see Chub's truck?" Betsy asked, breath coming in sharp gasps. She bent at the waist, hands on her knees.

Martha parted the bushes and looked out. Only a couple of cars were in Clover's lot, and Chub's truck wasn't among them. She shook her head.

"Martha, seriously, I can't keep running." Betsy straightened, her face red from the cold.

"Maybe Cy can hide you for a few days. He'd do it for me, I know he would." Martha placed a hand on her friend's arm.

Betsy shook her head. "No. Grant said he'd help me. I believe him."

"What? You don't even know the man."

Betsy blushed. "He'll help me."

Martha frowned. *Why is Betsy blushing? What happened between my friend and this handsome stranger?* "I don't know, Bets. Come on." She took

her friend's hand and led her to the back entrance of
Clover's.

Chapter Twenty-Six

Chub stormed back into Sal's. Clay and Pauline Dickerson were putting on their coats and talking to Sal, who stood behind the counter. Only a few customers remained and they too, hurried to don their coats when they caught sight of Chub.

He strode to the bar, slamming a ham-like fist on the polished surface. "I'm sick of your bullshit, Sal. Where's my wife?"

Clay and Pauline edged around the big man and hustled to the door. They left, a gust of arctic-like air sweeping through the room after them.

"I already told you. No idea. Go see O'Malley. File a missing persons report." He stacked the plates from the counter and wiped it clean. Sal looked up. He and Chub were the only ones in the place.

"You're lying. I know how to make you talk." Chub started around the counter, his face a dangerous shade of red, fists clenched.

The door opened again with a blast of icy air.

"I wouldn't do that if I were you," a voice said from the doorway.

Chub stopped in his tracks.

●●●●

I glanced at O'Malley. He sat back, a self-satisfied smirk on his face.

"See, Walleski. This bird can sing. And what a pretty song." He sat forward, swinging up and out of his chair in one fluid motion. "Where are those stones?" In two strides, he was in front of our prisoner, gripping him by the shirtfront. "We need those diamonds." He shook him.

"I can get 'em. I can get 'em. Lay off, man." Bud held up his manacled hands, trying to shield himself.

"You won't be retrieving them. We will." Johnson said, stepping forward. "We need a name. Phone number." He towered over Bud, pencil and small notepad in his hands. "Talk."

Bud swallowed, looking from one man to the other. "Connie Gaglione."

●●●●

Martha and Betsy let themselves in the back door of Clover's Mini Mart. They could hear voices coming from the front of the store. Creeping toward the curtain separating the storage area from the store, Martha parted the curtains and peeked out. Clay and Pauline stood at the counter, chatting with the clerk. She turned back to Betsy, finger to her lips.

"What?" Betsy whispered.

"Clay and Pauline are out there. We'll have to stay back here 'til they leave."

"This is driving me crazy," Betsy said, crouching beside her friend. "I want to go home and grab my things."

"Are you crazy? And risk Chub finding us there?" Martha hissed. She watched while Clay and Pauline left, the bell above the door tinkling as they closed it against the strong wind that had blown up. The clerk picked up a book from the counter and became immersed in it.

"Are we going to just stay here all day?" Betsy said, wringing her hands.

"No. Course not. Clay and Pauline just left. I think it's safe now." She pushed the curtains aside, and they went out into the nearest aisle. "Pick out something. Act natural."

Betsy eyed the selection of goodies. Twinkies, Ring Dings, Hostess Cupcakes, and Suzi-Qs. She grabbed a package of Twinkies and some cupcakes. Martha had a couple bags of chips in her hands.

"It's okay. Take a couple deep breaths," Martha said, noting her friend's pale face. "Let's go." Together they went to the front of the store.

●●●●

Two policemen came through the open door to Spike's room. He tensed. *What do they want? More questions?*

Smith, the cop who'd been in before, advanced to the bed. "It's your lucky day. You're outta here. The nurse'll be right in to help you get dressed."

"Where am I goin'?"

"Maine. We're gonna be your personal escort. Ain't that sweet?" the other cop said, laughing at his own joke. He grinned at Smith. They punched fists.

Spike looked from one to the other. "You kiddin' me? I have to ride all the way to fuckin' hickville with you two clowns?"

Smith lost his smile. "Watch who you call clowns, Spike. A lot can happen on those country roads." He touched the gun at his hip.

Spike saw the gesture and frowned. Maybe he'd better shut up with these two idiots.

A redheaded nurse bustled in and made shooing motions at the policemen. "Let's give the patient a little privacy, shall we, officers?" She checked her watch. "Say ten minutes?"

"We'll be right outside." Smith jerked his chin at the door. His partner followed him out.

●●●●

Grant walked into the restaurant, gun drawn. He saw Sal behind the counter gripping the edge like his life depended on it, Chub reaching for the owner's shirtfront.

"Back off, man. I won't ask again," Grant said.

"You again? This ain't none of your business, little man." Chub said, turning to face Grant. "Get lost." He raised his fists.

"You wouldn't want me to put a bullet in your fat ass." Grant cocked the gun, moving toward Chub. He aimed low and saw the big man follow the movement with his eyes.

Chub raised his hands, palms out. "This ain't over, pal. You'll be sorry."

"Leave," Grant said, motioning with the gun.

Chub kept his hands raised as he made his way to the door. His eyes never left Grant.

"Don't come back." Grant edged closer to the counter, glancing at Sal.

Chub pointed at Grant. "You're a dead man." He slammed the door behind him.

●●●●

I couldn't believe what I was hearing. *Connie bought the diamonds? How did she know about them?* Images flashed through my mind. Connie with the gun. Connie telling us she'd killed Clifton. All the new clothes she'd been wearing. *Was she involved with the smuggling ring? Was she part of it?*

I looked at O'Malley.

He stared at Kelly, fists clenched. "What kinda shit are you tryin' to feed us?"

Bud Kelly looked at each of us, a smirk on his face. He shrugged. "That's what that idiot at the pawn shop said. This dame, Connie, bought the rocks. Seemed to know all about 'em, too."

I turned to O'Malley. "I think it's time we had a talk with her."

169

The two Feebies moved as one toward the door. Alden stopped when we made to follow them. He held up his hand. "We'll take over from here."

I looked at O'Malley. He frowned and shook his head.

●●●●

Kent hurried to his room, making as little noise as possible. He glanced over his shoulder at a sudden movement below. Mrs. Shepherd stood at the bottom of the stairs staring up at him.

"I'm just getting my stuff. I'll pay what I owe you." He watched her step onto the first stair.

"You're leaving?"

He nodded.

"The police are looking for you. I think you'd better talk to them." She came up a few more stairs and stopped.

He shrugged. "Look, I just gotta go. Here's your money." He held out the bills he'd pulled from his wallet. "Take it." He handed it to her as she mounted the last few steps and came toward him.

She took the money from his hand and looked into his eyes. "They'll go easier on you if you just give yourself up."

Kent nodded. "I'll go talk to them."

●●●●

Martha and Betsy put their items on the counter and watched the clerk ring them up and put everything in a brown paper bag.

"Is that all, ladies?" The boy pushed the dark hair from his eyes and smiled shyly at them. He hefted the bag and held it out.

Martha nodded. "Thanks." She took the sack from him, smiling in return. She heard Betsy gasp. She swiveled toward her. "What?" Betsy had turned white as the snow on the ground outside the door.

Martha looked where Betsy was pointing. Chub was coming toward the door. Her eyes locked with his. She dropped the bag.

●●●●

Spike winced with each bump the wheelchair hit. The cop pushing the chair seemed to take great pleasure in his discomfort. Once outside, the sun was blinding, reflecting off the snow that covered the lawns of the hospital. Spike squinted, wishing he had his sunglasses. He raised his hand to shield his eyes.

"Don't worry, pal. Where you're goin', you won't need sunglasses," the other cop following them said. The two cops laughed.

Spike saw a cruiser up ahead. His jailors steered him toward it and hit another bump. Spike's teeth clicked together with a sharp clack. It made his jaws tingle. He closed his eyes, dreading the ride ahead.

●●●●

Grant lowered the gun and came around the counter. He tucked the gun in the back of his waistband and pulled his coat over it.

"You okay?"

Sal nodded. "Yeah. Thanks. Don't know what would've happened if you hadn't come in when you did."

"I think you oughta call the cops."

Sal shook his head. "Got 'em all in his back pocket. O'Malley included. Chub's got a lotta dough and knows just whose palms to grease."

"Are you kidding? That idiot? Where's he get his money?" Grant went back around the counter and took a seat.

Sal followed and sat beside him. "Won the lottery. Can you beat that?"

Grant shook his head and stood. "Look, are you okay if I leave?" He watched the other man's face. "I've got to find Betsy before he does."

Sal started. "She's with my wife. They're at the bed and breakfast."

Grant shook his head. "I was just there. They left. Lady that runs the place sent them down a path through the woods. Know where it comes out?"

Sal nodded. "Clover's," he said with a gulp.

Chapter Twenty-Seven

I watched Johnson and Alden leave the room, escorting Bud to a cell. O'Malley leaned back in his chair and opened the bottom drawer of his desk, placing a bottle and two shot glasses on the blotter. He poured a generous dollop in each and handed me one.

"We need this, Walleski," he said, downing his. "I don't think they'll get anything from Connie. Do you?"

I gulped the liquid fire and set the glass on the desk, shaking my head. "Nah." I looked at my watch. "Give 'em another five minutes. They'll be back."

O'Malley smiled and refilled our glasses. He raised his. "Here's to small-town law."

I touched my glass to his and downed the liquor, the warmth spreading through me.

"By the way, did you find anything at Dexter's?"

"Nothin.' I think that kid's got the other stones."

"Other stones?" I asked. "How many were there?"

"Four." O'Malley shifted in his seat. He looked guilty.

"How do you know there were four?"

He rolled a pencil on the blotter, avoiding my eyes. "I was there."

"In the woods? At the snowman?" I sat forward, slamming the glass on the desk.

He nodded, looking up. "I'd been watching him for a while. Knew he was involved in something big. I followed him that night and saw him with the carrot nose of the snowman. The dumb ass shook the diamonds into his palm right there in the open. Can you believe it?" He shook his head.

"Did you tell the Feebies?"

"No way. This is my case. I'm not gonna have no city boys get in my way." The bottle and two glasses disappeared. O'Malley closed the drawer, nodding toward the door. "They're coming back."

I heard footsteps. The door opened and Agent Alden stepped in, followed by his partner.

"She wouldn't say a thing. Just shook her head." Alden leaned against the wall, eyeing O'Malley. "Think you'll do any better?" He glanced at Johnson, who stood by the window looking out.

O'Malley shook his head. "Might talk to Cy though." He tilted his head toward me.

Johnson turned. "Go ahead. Good luck." He gestured at the door.

"I got a better idea," O'Malley said, leaning forward. "Bring her in and get that scumbag back here. Maybe between the two of 'em we'll get somewhere."

"That could work," Johnson said, turning back to face us.

"Worth a try," I said, reaching for the doorknob.

●●●●

Chub pushed open the door to Clover's and stepped inside. Martha pushed Betsy behind her.

"Get outta my way, Martha. Betsy, come on. We're goin' home." He grabbed Martha's arm, pushing her aside.

"I don't want any trouble, mister," the young clerk squeaked.

Chub rounded on him. "Shut up, asshole. I'm gettin' my wife."

Martha stepped in front of Chub. "She doesn't want to go with you, Chub."

"Oh yeah? Betsy? Get your ass over here. I'm not gonna ask again." He reached around Martha and grabbed Betsy's arm, pulling her to him.

"I don't want to go home. I want a divorce," Betsy shrieked, trying to get away.

"No wife of mine leaves me unless she's six feet under." Chub dragged her to the door.

"Let her go!" Martha screamed. She grabbed a can from a nearby display and hurled it at him. It hit his chin with a resounding thwack.

"You bitch! You're gonna pay for that." He spit out a tooth.

The clerk stepped from behind the counter, phone in hand. "I'm calling the police."

"Go right ahead," Chub said, rubbing his free hand across his bloody mouth. "See where that gets ya." Yanking Betsy by the arm, he backed out of the store.

●●●●

The ride to Maine seemed to go on forever. Each bump sent a fresh wave of pain through Spike's head, and his injured arms throbbed. *Will this nightmare never end?* He watched the countryside speed by and saw the sign announcing they had finally entered Maine. Tall pines, their branches covered with snow, bowed and swayed in the wind. Spike shivered. The interior of the car was none too warm and his feet were like ice.

"Ready for show time, Spike?" Smith asked, looking in the rearview mirror. He chuckled, and the cop in the passenger seat joined in.

Spike glared at them. Assholes. Did they really think they were funny? He wondered how Bud was doing. *And Kent. Where is he?* He looked out the window again and saw they were entering a town, a few stores lining the road. He hoped they'd stop and get something to eat.

As if reading his mind, the other cop turned to look at him. "Hungry?"

Spike nodded.

The cop laughed. "Gee, too bad you're not gettin' anything." He laughed and the two cops bumped fists.

Smith turned into a McDonald's. He headed for the drive-thru and lowered the window, turning to his companion. "Whatta ya want?"

"Burger and fries and a medium Coke." He turned and smirked at Spike.

"I'll have the same," Spike said from the rear.

"Right," Smith said. He spoke into the speaker, giving their order, then pulled up to the next window. A girl slid open the glass and took his money, passing a couple of bags to him.

Spike's mouth watered when they opened the bag and he got a whiff of the contents. He was ravenous.

Smith steered the car into a parking spot and killed the engine.

The rustle of the bag and the delicious smells were driving Spike crazy. *Are those fuckers really going to starve me?*

"Sorry there isn't enough for you, Spike," Smith said, talking through a mouthful of food. The other cop guffawed, slurping his Coke loudly.

Spike leaned back against the seat and closed his eyes. *Bastards.*

●●●●

Grant, with Sal on his heels, slammed through the door to Clover's. The startled clerk, eyes like saucers, dropped the phone he was holding.

"Was Chub here?" Grant asked the boy.

"Big guy?" the kid asked, retrieving the phone.

Sal stepped up to the register. "Yeah. How about a couple of women? One blond, the other dark blond?"

The young clerk nodded. "The guy grabbed the blonde and tore outta here. He shoved her in a truck. Don't know where the other lady went."

"Shit!" Grant clenched his fists. "Where do you think he'd take her? Home?"

Sal shook his head. "Crazy fuck. I'm gonna kill him if he touches my wife."

"Did you call the cops?" Grant asked.

The kid shook his head. "He just laughed at me. Said it wouldn't do any good."

"Gimme the phone," Sal demanded. He took it and dialed.

●●●●

I made my way into the room on my crutches, and stared at Connie. She sat slumped on the cot in her cell, face turned away. I noticed a tray of untouched food on the floor at her feet.

"Connie?" My voice sounded cold as ice, even to my ears.

She turned at the sound of my voice. "Cy. I'm so sorry. I wish I could take it all back." She got up and came to the bars, grasping them. Her eyes brimmed with unshed tears.

"Come on. We need to talk to you." I took the keys O'Malley had thrown me and unlocked her cell.

"I didn't kill him," she whispered, easing through the opened cell door.

"What?" I moved closer and taking my hand from my crutch, grasped her arm. "What kind of bullshit are you trying to hand me now?"

"I didn't kill Clifton, Kent did."

"Kent?" I stared at the woman I once thought I'd known.

She nodded. "I was there. I saw him do it. He took that carrot from the snowman and rammed it into Clifton's ear."

177

"Stop. You need to tell this to O'Malley." I motioned her ahead of me with my crutch, and followed her to O'Malley's office. I couldn't believe what I'd just heard.

The bald-headed kid was already in the room, slouched in his chair. He glared at Connie and then me.

"Come on in, Connie. Join us. Have a seat." O'Malley gestured to a chair next to the manacled prisoner. The two FBI agents stood, arms folded, eyes following every move.

"Miss Gaglione, tell us what you know about the diamonds." Johnson stepped in front of her and looked in her eyes.

"Wha . . . what diamonds?"

"Don't play stupid with us, Connie. We know you went to the pawnshop and got the diamonds. How did you know about them?" Johnson crouched down, hands resting on the chair arms.

Tears ran down her cheeks. She shuddered, closing her eyes. "The man who owns the shop is my cousin. He thought I might like them," she whispered.

"Bullshit!" Alden spat, advancing on her. She shrank back in her chair.

"All right. Hold on." I lowered myself into a chair. "Tell them what you told me outside." She looked over at me.

"I saw Kent kill Clifton." She turned toward O'Malley. "He took that carrot from the snowman and rammed it into Clifton's ear."

"Shit! He's one crazy dude." Bud said, pulling on his handcuffs.

"Quiet." O'Malley scowled at the prisoner then turned his attention to Connie. He hunched forward. "Okay, did you hear anything before that happened?"

She nodded. "They were arguing. I heard Cliff telling Kent to go home. Saying something about a case and how Kent was in danger if he stayed."

"Where's the kid now?" Alden asked.

"I don't know." Connie motioned to the box of tissues on O'Malley's desk. He leaned forward, offering her one.

"I can answer that," a voice said from the opened door. Smitty stood there, phone in hand.

"Well?" O'Malley said, brows raised.

"Just got off the phone with Mrs. Shepherd. Seems her missing tenant came back. Guess who? Kent Blake."

Chapter Twenty-Eight

Bud sat enjoying the show. *At least someone else is in the hot seat for now,* he thought. *The bitch deserves whatever they dish out to her.* He chuckled under his breath. *Wonder what she did with those diamonds.*

The two FBI agents turned his way.

Shit.

"Where did you get the diamonds?" the one called Alden asked.

"From that kid. Kent."

"Where'd he get them?" the other agent asked, before Alden could continue.

Bud shrugged. "Said he got 'em off his old man."

"Dexter?" O'Malley asked, drumming his fingers on the desktop.

"That his old man's name?"

O'Malley nodded. "What else did he say?"

"That he iced his brother at midnight. Then did his old man." Bud smiled and licked his lips. This was fun. Goading the assholes.

"*He* killed Dexter?" O'Malley asked.

Bud laughed. "Yup."

●●●●

Chub trod on the pedal, spinning the wheels, shooting ice and slush from them. He fishtailed out of Clover's parking lot and onto the road. Betsy screeched and clung to the door handle. He smiled, envisioning what he was going to do to her once they got home.

"Stop this car. Now!" Betsy demanded.

"Shut the fuck up, bitch. You ain't goin' nowhere but back home where you belong." Chub gave the truck some more gas and slid down the road toward home. He reached over and backhanded her across the face. She fell heavily against the door. He heard the sharp crack as her head connected with the glass.

"I hate you."

Chub looked over at her. Blood ran from her split lips, and one eye was starting to swell.

She sobbed.

Not so pretty now. Wait 'til we get home. He laughed.

●●●●

Grant watched Sal talking low into the phone. He'd turned his back on him and the young clerk who stood wringing his hands. Grant shifted from one foot to the other. *We need to leave,* he thought.

"I'm sorry, mister. I didn't know what to do. That guy had murder in his eyes."

"It's okay, kid. You did the right thing. He's dangerous." Grant patted the boy's shoulder.

Sal turned back to them. "The police are coming. Tell them what you told us," he said to the clerk.

Grant touched the gun in his waistband and motioned to Sal. "Let's go."

●●●●

O'Malley jumped up. "Let's go get that little fuck."

"Not so fast." Johnson held up his hand. "You stay here, O'Malley, and take care of them." He nodded toward the two prisoners. "We'll take Walleski with us."

"Now wait just a minute," O'Malley sputtered.

"Why do we need him?" Alden pointed at me.

"He's from here. Knows everybody. It'll make it easier." Johnson opened the door.

Alden looked at me and frowned. "Whatever."

I looked back at Connie slumped in her chair and Bud, who eyed me, a sneer on his face. "Chief?" I turned to O'Malley.

O'Malley grimaced, nodding. "Go ahead, Walleski. Get that little prick."

I smiled. "Will do."

◆◆◆◆

Grant followed Sal out to his pickup. He didn't wait to be told and jumped in the passenger seat. He noticed Sal's hands shaking as he tried to shove the key in the ignition. "Want me to drive?" Grant asked, leaning forward to stare out the window.

"No. I'm okay." The truck roared to life and Sal slammed it into drive. They tore out of the lot, snow flying from the tires. "I think that dumb shit'll take her home. He's not afraid of anybody. He makes his own laws." Sal tightened his grip on the wheel and gave the truck more gas.

"He'll be afraid of me when he's staring down the barrel of my gun," Grant said, pulling the weapon from his waistband.

Sal glanced over at him. "I been meanin' to ask you. Where'd you get that?"

"I never leave home without it." Grant checked the safety.

"Good. Cause we're gonna need it." Sal steered the truck around a bend in the road and took the turnoff for Chub's street. "There's the house." Sal nodded to a neat cape with blue shutters. "And his truck. Just like I said."

Grant saw Chub's beast of a truck parked in the driveway. *The balls of the guy.* He really did think he was above the law.

Sal pulled over to the side of the road and killed the engine. He looked at Grant. "Ready?"

"As I'll ever be." He released the safety on the gun and followed Sal toward the house.

●●●●

Martha raced through the woods toward Mrs. Shepherd's. Her lungs were aching when she burst from the trees and flew to the back door. Grateful to find it unlocked, she threw herself inside and collapsed on the floor. Her chest heaved as she fought to regain her breath. *Did Mrs. Shepherd call the police?* Dear God, she hoped so.

Once her heart stopped pounding and she could take in a few deep breaths, she stood, listening. All was quiet. She made her way down the hall and peeked through the door to the front foyer. No one seemed to be around. She slipped into the room and stopped. *What was that sound?*

Someone was talking on the phone in the kitchen, just to her left. She heard the woman's voice rise as if in panic. *Mrs. Shepherd?* She moved toward the sound. The voice stopped. Martha heard footsteps coming her way. She froze.

●●●●

Kent got in the car and started the engine. He thought he saw someone come from the woods and run toward the back of the building. A woman? He killed the engine and got out. *What is going on?* He tightened his scarf and went back to the front door, letting himself in. All was quiet. No one around. He hesitated, listening. Did he hear voices? Yes, coming from the back of the house. Kent edged down the hallway, careful not to make any noise. He saw a woman, back to him, moving toward the kitchen. He followed, a board creaking under his foot. The woman froze.

Shit! Kent ducked into a room on his right. He eased the door closed behind him.

●●●●

Chub flung Betsy into an armchair in the living room. "Stay there. Don't you dare move. I'll be right back." He stomped up the stairs to the bedroom and pulled the thick leather belt from the hanger in the closet. He held it in his hands and snapped it a few times, liking the sound it made and thinking about the whipping he was going to give her.

A sound from downstairs made him pause. *Is that little bitch defying me? Trying to get away?* The sound of the front door opening had him howling with rage. He tore down the stairs and stopped dead. There in his living room stood Sal and that bastard, Grant. And the stranger held a gun. Pointed at Chub.

"What the fuck? Get outta my house. Ain't no business of yours." He turned to look at Betsy cowering in the chair where he'd left her. "You let these assholes in?"

Betsy shook her head.

"We let ourselves in, you bastard. You're not going to hurt her again." Grant leveled the gun, aiming at Chub's chest.

"That's right, Chub. It's over." Sal straightened. He beckoned to Betsy. "Come on. We're leaving, and you're coming with us."

With a roar, Chub threw himself at Grant. The gun went off.

Chapter Twenty-Nine

Johnson turned the wheel of his dark sedan and pulled into a parking spot at the Gammil's Point Bed and Breakfast. There, not fifty feet away, sat a red Trans Am.

"That's the kid's car," Alden said, sitting forward, grasping the dashboard.

"Yup. The license plate's right," I said, straining to catch a glimpse of the tail end of the car from the back seat of Johnson's ride. I noticed there weren't many cars in the lot. *Good. We didn't need any innocent people getting in the way.*

Johnson shut off the engine. "Come on. Lead the way, Walleski. I assume you know the person who owns this place."

"Mrs. Shepherd. Nice lady." I unfolded myself from the back seat. Alden held the door.

They drew their weapons. I did the same.

"You go around to the back, Walleski," Johnson said, motioning with his gun. "Alden, you head to the side. Over there." He pointed to the woods by the building.

I discarded my crutches and, limping and in pain, circled the bed and breakfast, arriving at the back door. Not seeing anyone, I crept up the stairs. My heart was pounding so hard I thought it would burst from my chest. My throat was tight, my mouth dry. Slowly, I eased open the door and peered inside. All clear. Or so I thought. A noise to my right. I swung toward the sound, the gun held in front of me.

A door on the opposite wall opened. Martha stepped into the room. Her eyes widened when she saw me.

I held a finger to my lips and motioned her over with the gun. She flew across the room and grabbed my arm. I lowered my weapon.

"Cy. What are you doing here?" she whispered.

"Have you seen the kid who works at Clover's? We got a tip he was here."

"Kent? The one everybody's talking about?"

"Yeah. I'm with the FBI guys who're looking for him, too."

"FBI? Where are they?" She went to the window and drew back the curtain.

"Never mind. Have you seen Kent?"

"No. Who called?" She turned to look at me.

"Mrs. Shepherd. Where's she?"

"I don't know. I heard voices. That's why I came in here." She wrung her hands. "What's happening, Cy?"

"Not sure, Martha. Go outside. Find the two agents and stay with them. I gotta look for Kent." I guided her to the door. "Go."

◆●◆●

"What the fuck!" Chub fell heavily and rolled to his side, grabbing his injured arm. Blood oozed from between his fingers. "Ya shot me."

Grant stood over him, gun aimed at his face. "And don't think I won't again." He had the satisfaction of seeing the big brute's face pale.

"Police are on their way," Sal said, closing his phone and putting an arm around a shaking Betsy.

"What's going to happen to him now?" Betsy whispered, looking into Sal's eyes. "Will he go to jail?"

"He better," Grant said. "I plan on pressing charges." He looked down at Chub.

"Jail!" Chub choked out. "You two broke into my place. And you shot me!" He glared up at Grant. "I'll get the best lawyers money can buy. I won't see a day of jail time." He pulled a handkerchief from his pocket and pressed it against the wound. "But you will."

The wail of a siren grew louder. Sal pulled the curtains back and looked out the window. "Cops are here and an ambulance, too. I'll let 'em in."

Betsy clung to Sal. "I'm coming with you."

He nodded.

Kent heard the sound of a man's voice coming from the room the woman had just entered. *Where have I heard that voice before?* He crept to the door and listened. He could hear the low murmur of their voices. The sound of a chair being pulled back. Footsteps coming his way. He scurried back to the room he'd come from and ducked inside.

His breath came in shallow gasps, his heart was racing. He could feel the blood pounding in his ears. Someone moved down the hall, headed his way. Kent pulled the gun from his waistband and released the safety. He gripped it with shaking hands. Holding his breath, he waited behind the door, silently willing the person to go past the room. The footsteps stopped outside the door.

Spike saw a sign off to their right. Gammil's Point. They were here. He looked out at the places they passed and focused on a brick building they headed toward. The sign out front read Police in large block letters. They pulled into a spot not far from the front door. Spike gulped. He could feel his palms grow moist.

Smith got out and stretched. The other cop, the one Spike thought looked like a rooster with a tangled mop of red hair, stuck his head in the door and smirked at him.

"Okay, Spike, get out."

Smith stomped over and before Spike could put a foot out, grabbed him by one of his injured arms and jerked him toward the door. "Come on, time's a wastin'."

Spike yelped.

The two cops laughed.

"What's going on out here?" A uniformed officer stepped from the building and glared at Smith and his partner. "Need some help?"

"Got it under control. We're here to see Chief O'Malley. Got someone I think he's waiting to see." Smith said, nudging Spike forward.

"Bring him in," the officer said, stepping aside to let them enter.

Spike looked at this new cop and his shiny black shoes. *Another bozo,* he thought. The cops pulled him roughly toward the door.

●●●●

Tack pulled up to Clover's and killed the engine and the siren. He got out and drew his weapon, making his way toward the front door. A frightened face peered from the window. A moment later the front door opened. The clerk stood on the threshold, a phone in his hand.

"You okay, kid?" Tack asked.

The boy nodded.

"Anybody there with you?"

"No. They left."

"Who left?" Tack lowered the gun, holstering it.

"Mr. Sal and some other guy. They went after a crazy dude in a truck."

"Okay, kid. You sure you're okay?"

The clerk smiled. "Yeah."

Just then the radio in the cruiser squawked to life. Tack hurried to answer. He slid behind the wheel and picked up the receiver. "Unit 101 here. Over."

"Unit 101, 10-10 at 95 Seacrest Lane. Backup requested. Over."

"Right. On my way." Tack ended the call and turned on the siren. He slewed out of the lot, spraying slush and ice.

●●●●

I saw someone slip into a room off to my left. I held my gun ready and, keeping my steps light, made my way toward the room. The pain from the wound in my foot had me biting my lip to keep from making any noise. Someone was just beyond the closed door, I was sure of it.

"Mr. Walleski, thank goodness!" Mrs. Shepherd came in the front door and hurried toward me. She drew up short when she noticed the gun. "Wha . . ."

I came up beside her. "Who's in that room?" I whispered, nodding toward the door.

"No one. It's vacant."

"I just saw someone go in there."

Her eyes widened.

"Go outside. Find Martha. Stay with her."

She nodded and slipped by me.

Again, I moved toward the room. Gun drawn. Once outside the room, I stopped.

"Come out with your hands up." I stood off to the side, my foot throbbing. A shot rang out, a bullet piercing the wooden panel of the door. I shifted to the left and inched closer. "It's no use, Kent. There's two FBI agents here with me. You got nowhere to go."

"Screw that. If I come out, I'm a dead man anyway."

"Come on. I'll bring you in myself." I tried the knob.

"Get back," he screamed, firing another round. The bullet splintered the door inches from my head. I jumped back.

"Don't do anything foolish, son. Come out."

Suddenly the door burst open and the boy was on me. His gun flashed, the sound loud in my ears. I

189

felt a sharp pain in my side, and my foot was numb. I fired back. Kent collapsed on top of me. The silence in the hallway was broken by the sound of running feet.

Chapter Thirty

"Chief O'Malley. Nice to meet you." The tall cop held out his hand. "I'm Smith. This is West."

O'Malley stepped forward and they shook. He looked toward the specter that stood between the two officers, both arms in casts. From the bright orange Mohawk and multi-pierced body to the leather clothes he wore, O'Malley thought he'd never seen such a freak.

"This here's Spike," said West. He pushed the prisoner toward O'Malley. "I'm sure he'll be a font of information." He laughed.

"Let's go to my office," O'Malley said, gesturing toward the back of the room. "I got someone waitin' to see old Spike." He grinned at the prisoner and led the way.

❖❖❖

The two FBI agents knelt by my side. "Shit, Walleski. You hit?" Alden asked. He felt for a pulse on Kent and gently eased him off me.

I nodded. "My side. Is he . . .?"

Alden nodded. "He's gone." He flipped open his cell and dialed. "We've got a DOA and an officer down." He turned to me. "What's the address here?"

I told him, wincing when Johnson pulled open my jacket and shirt and applied pressure to the wound with a handkerchief he pulled from his pocket. Out of the corner of my eye, I saw Martha and Mrs. Shepherd standing nearby.

Alden rose. "Are you the owner?" he asked Mrs. Shepherd.

She nodded.

"Grab some towels, would you?"

"Of course." She scurried off.

Martha knelt beside me. "Oh, Cy." She turned. "Is he going to be all right?" she asked, looking up at Johnson.

"Yeah. Lucky for him, the bullet just grazed him."

Doris Shepherd returned, arms laden with towels. She held them out. "This enough?"

"Yeah. Plenty." Johnson waved toward Martha. "Grab one and apply pressure when I take away the handkerchief, okay?"

Martha rose and taking a towel, did as she was told.

I smiled at her. "It's okay, Martha, I think I'll make it." I chuckled then grunted, pain shooting through my side.

A siren sounded from outside. Reinforcements were here. I closed my eyes.

♦●♦●

Connie and Bud exchanged glances when the door opened and O'Malley entered, followed by two uniformed officers leading a strange-looking guy. Connie saw a spark of recognition in Bud's eyes. They did know each other.

Once the newcomers were seated, all eyes shifted to them. Connie squirmed in her seat, feeling like a bug under a magnifying glass. She looked over at Bud again. He lounged back against his chair, seemingly at ease. *How can he be so calm?* She pulled at her manacled wrists, the metal chafing her skin.

O'Malley sat back in his chair and stared at her. "Well, Connie? Know this freak?"

Connie shifted again, trying to get comfortable in the wooden chair. Her back hurt and she needed the bathroom. She gulped. "No. I've never seen him before." She looked at Bud, who returned her glance with a smirk.

"I know you know each other," O'Malley said to Bud and the tattooed freak. "So who wants to go first?" He leaned forward and rested his elbow on the desktop.

One of the cops cleared his throat. "Mind if we take off, O'Malley? We're done here," the one who'd introduced himself as Smith said.

Connie looked at the two Massachusetts cops, who seemed uncomfortable in the small room. She smiled, thinking they looked like a couple of misfits. One so big and the other dwarfed by his companion. Smith and West. So close to Smith and Wesson.

"Yeah, go on. We're all set here. Right, folks?" O'Malley guffawed.

Connie looked at the new prisoner. He sat slouched in his chair, arms resting lightly in his lap. He, too, seemed unconcerned with his current plight. She watched the two Mass policemen leave, the closing of the door sounding like a death sentence.

O'Malley leaned back in his chair and put his feet up on the desk. He glared at the two men.

Connie felt her chest tighten. Would either of them talk?

●●●●

Tack pulled over to the side of the road at Chub's house. A cruiser and an ambulance were already there, a couple of attendants wheeling out a stretcher with someone on it. Tack got out and followed the path to meet them. When he drew abreast of them, he noticed who the wounded man was.

Chub rose up on his elbows, hooded eyes glaring angrily. "Whatta you want?" he snarled. "Come to gloat, so ya can run to Walleski and have a good laugh?" He grunted, collapsing back onto the gurney.

"What happened here, Chub?" Tack watched the men maneuver the stretcher into the back of the vehicle. He saw them adjust Chub's IV and check his vitals.

"Damned bastards thought they could bust in my house and take my wife." Chub shouted from inside. "Go arrest them."

"We've got to get him to the hospital, Detective," one of the attendants said, jumping down to close the door. "You can talk to him once they're done with him there."

"Sure," Tack shrugged. He watched the man jump in the front seat and pull out of the driveway. He turned to go inside.

●◆●◆

They tended to my wound at the hospital. I was lucky, they told me. A few inches to the right and it could've been bad. Johnson and Alden had followed the ambulance to the hospital and were waiting when I came out. I hobbled to their car, holding my side. The doctor had given me something for the pain, with a prescription to fill for home. He also checked my foot and replaced the bandage with a new one. In all the excitement, I'd reopened the wound. It ached like hell. I drew alongside the passenger door of the car.

Alden lowered the window. "Get in. We'll give you a ride home."

I got in back and leaned against the seat. What a horrible Christmas this had turned into. I sat forward. "Take me back to the station. Two cops from Mass brought Spike up. Seems he, Bud and Connie have a lot to tell us."

"About time something went right." Alden turned to grin at me.

●●●●

Sal sat next to Betsy on the sofa. "Can I get you anything? Cup of tea? A soda?"

Betsy shook her head. "Where's Martha?"

"It's okay. She called me. Doris Shepherd is driving her home. They got that kid. One from Clover's. Cy shot him."

Betsy's eyes widened. "Is Cy okay?"

"Kid shot him, too, but he'll be fine." Sal checked the screen of his cell and shoved it into his pocket. No calls.

"What's gonna happen, Sal? He'll be back, won't he?" She turned tear-filled eyes his way.

Grant left his post at the front door. He hurried over to the couch, sinking down on Betsy's other side. "You'll never have to be with him again, honey." He took her hand.

"You don't know him. He's got a lot of pull. Especially with the police." She shook her head. "He'll come home and everything will go back the way it was."

"Not if I can help it." Grant rubbed her trembling hands.

She smiled at him, tears gathering at the corners of her eyes.

●●●●

We pulled up to the station, and I made my painful way out of the car. Johnson and Alden waited for me, with my crutches, and together we mounted the steps into the station.

Smitty nodded to me and jerked his chin toward O'Malley's office. "I told him you were here."

The three of us went down the hall. I heard the murmur of voices coming from O'Malley's inner sanctum. The two agents stepped behind me. I knocked.

"Come in, Walleski. I hope you got good news."

Johnson opened the door and we went in. Connie and Bud were where we'd left them and a new prisoner sat slouched on the opposite side of the room. Spike. I remembered the hideous hair and the desecration of his face with all those pieces of metal. He looked too comfortable, even though both arms wore casts. Connie was awkwardly gripping a glass of water in her manacled hands. Bud was eyeing a package of cigarettes on the desktop.

"Grab a couple of chairs, boys. Make yourselves comfortable." O'Malley shook out a cigarette and lit it, pulling in a lungful of smoke and exhaling toward Bud. He chuckled. "Want one, kid?"

Bud nodded, staring at O'Malley, a hungry look on his face.

"Too bad." He blew a smoke ring toward the ceiling.

"Okay, O'Malley. Cut it out. We need to separate them." Alden leaned forward, glaring in O'Malley's direction.

I eased into a chair.

"Sure. Smitty?" He dropped his feet to the floor and crushed out his cigarette.

"Yeah, boss?" Smitty poked his head around the corner like he'd been eavesdropping.

"You and whoever else is covering take Bud and Spike here and lock 'em up."

"Sure thing." Smitty hurried out to the front desk. A moment later, he returned with a stocky officer at his heels. They hustled off the two guys.

Connie looked my way, her face ghost-white. Her hands shook, spilling water from the glass.

"Could I have a minute alone with Connie?" I asked O'Malley. Johnson and Alden pressed forward like a couple of wild dogs. I could almost feel their hot breath on my neck.

"Not a good idea," Johnson said, moving closer.

O'Malley held up a hand. "I trust Walleski. Let's give him a minute. What can it hurt?"

The two agents grumbled, but agreed to let me have my five minutes of fame. They left the room with O'Malley.

I pulled my chair closer to Connie, wincing. "Okay, Connie. We haven't got much time. Start from the beginning. Don't leave anything out."

She nodded and began to speak.

Chapter Thirty-One

Connie told me everything, including the fact that Grant Parsons was the ringleader of the smuggling gang. She recounted how he and his partner Pedro worked the resorts down in Palm Beach, Florida, in the winter months, cozying up to rich widows and stealing their jewels. They then pried the stones from their settings and sent the jewels up here to Gammil's Point, where Dexter placed them in a hollowed out carrot nose of a snowman in the deserted yard of the Pike place. Connie said she'd retrieve them and send them down to her cousin in Massachusetts to sell in his pawn shop.

It was a nice little setup 'til the FBI caught wind of it. Connie believed Clifton had been asked to investigate, and Kent had seen him, following him out to the snowman. There she'd witnessed Kent killing his brother with the carrot.

●●●●

A couple of months had gone by and the snow was starting to melt down, a few brave shoots straining for the sun. Connie will probably get a few years knocked off her sentence for her help in rounding up Grant and Pedro, but that's it. I wasn't happy with that, but what can you do? I'd just have to live with it.

Chub got out on bail and went back home, but Betsy left him anyway to join her mother, back in Massachusetts, where she'd been brought up. I heard a divorce was in the works.

Martha and Sal talk about the excitement whenever anybody shows an interest.

And the most surprising thing of all? Mrs. Shepherd's place is doing a booming business and she's dating someone. Never too old for love.

Bud and Spike will be doing time. It'll be a long while before Bud gets out, I'm sure.

O'Malley offered me my old job back, but I turned him down. I kind of like the status quo. On my own.

Chapter Thirty-Two

It was April and I was growing restless after a long snowy winter. Too keyed up to work on my manuscript, I made a decision. A trip down to Brewster to talk with Simone's parents was what I needed. To find out more about her life and Clifton's. Put the past to rest once and for all.

I packed a small bag and dialed the Blake's number. The phone was picked up on the third ring.

"Hello?" a female voice answered.

"Mrs. Blake?"

"Yes. Who's this?"

"Hi. It's Cy Walleski. Remember me?" I grasped the phone like a lifeline, my fingers almost going numb.

"Of course. How are you, Cy?"

"Not so good. Could I come to see you? And your husband, of course." I held my breath, waiting for her answer.

I heard her sigh. "We're still in shock over losing them all. Both grandsons and dear Simone. Our only child," she sobbed.

"I know. That's why I need to see you. To find out more about them. What I missed. Can you understand?"

"Yes, dear. I think I do. When did you want to come down?"

"Now. I've got my bag packed."

"Fine. I'll see you soon."

I heard the click of the receiver. I looked out the window at the branches of my maple tree swaying in the wind. A last bit of melting snow plopped from a nearby evergreen. The ticking of the hall clock sounded loud to my ears. I needed to get a move on if I wanted to get there at a reasonable hour. I grabbed my bag and locked the front door.

My old car sat in its usual spot, a fine layer of late April snow dusting its surface. This had sure been a record year for snowfall. Even the old-timers were talking about it. I got in and started the engine. Pulling from my drive, I headed to the Cape.

●●●●

My visit with the Blakes was bittersweet, them telling me story after story and me listening. I spent the better part of the day with them. When I left, with promises to return, I was dog-tired. Worn out. Both physically and emotionally. On impulse, I decided to look for someplace to spend the night.

As I drove down the picturesque streets of Brewster, I wasn't seeing the quaint beauty of the place, but the faces of the Blakes as I'd left them: hers, tear-stained and broken; his, solemn and devoid of emotion. Our lives had been changed forever. I stopped fighting the urge and pulled over. I shook a smoke from the pack I kept in the glove compartment and lit up. I took a huge breath and held the smoke in for what seemed like forever, exhaling in a rush. The buzz I felt eased the pain and heartache. If only for a while.

I finished my cigarette and continued on, scanning the roadside for an inn or bed and breakfast. A large gray building on my right caught my eye. The sign out front read The Beached Whale. How appropriate. A small vacancy sign hung from the larger sign. I made up my mind and turned into the driveway, tires crunching clamshells in their wake. The place was homey with a large farmer's porch in front, a wooden swing on one side, and two rockers on the other

I parked in the lot out behind the place and came around to the front. Climbing the steps, I saw a woman's straw hat and a basket of shells on one of the chairs. I rang the bell and took in a breath. The tang of salt air stirred my senses, bringing with it an overwhelming urge to walk the beach. I hadn't done that in a long time. Too long.

The door opened. A woman in tight jeans and a red plaid shirt looked me over carefully before speaking. Her hair was the color of beach sand on a bright summer day. Finely arched brows rose as if a question were forming on those lush red lips. Eyes the color of melted chocolate moved back and forth as she read my face like a book.

"Are you all right?" she asked.

I shook my head, realizing I must have zoned out for a moment.

"Do you want a room?" Her voice was soft and very feminine. She continued her scrutiny of me.

"I saw the sign. Out front." I suddenly felt like an awkward teen, standing here on a porch in the fading light of an afternoon in Massachusetts.

"How rude of me. Of course. Come in." She stepped aside for me to enter. I followed her to a large desk by a back wall of a massive entryway. She stepped behind it and drew out a ledger. She turned it around for me, pointing to the page. "Would you sign in for me, please?" She handed me a pen. "Room four is open. It's got a lovely view of the ocean. It's not a long walk from here, if you don't mind the cold."

"I'll take it," I said, stifling a yawn.

"Great. It's ninety-five a night and there's a bathroom just across the hall. Just go up those stairs," she gestured to her left, "and your room is the second on the right. Cash or charge? We take MasterCard and Visa." She said the last in a rush, with a sweet smile and the hint of a dimple in her cheek.

What I'd give to be thirty again. I felt so old, and defeated.

She ran my card, and turned the ledger back to look at my signature. "Here you are, Mr. Walleski," she said, handing me my card and a key.

"Hey, call me Cy. Everyone does." I smiled at her. She sure was easy on the eyes.

"Cy. Short for?"

"Cyrus. Nobody ever calls me that. If they did, I probably wouldn't answer." I laughed in spite of my heavy heart. I felt at ease with this wisp of a woman.

"Cy. I like that. It fits. Not Cyrus. I'm Joanie Parks, by the way. Owner of this place." She held out her hand.

"Nice to meet you, Miss Parks." I looked into those velvety eyes and took her small hand in mine. Her fingers were long and tapered, the nails painted a soft shade of pink. She really was a knockout.

"Call me Joanie, please."

"Great." I shuffled my feet, feeling awkward again.

"Oh, here's a key to the front door, if you decide to take that walk." She smiled at me, and placed another key in my hand.

I didn't notice a wedding band. "Thanks, I just might."

I headed up the stairs to my room. It had a nautical theme with lots of shells in little baskets and paintings of the sea on the blue walls. I sat on the edge of the four-poster bed and let my thoughts wash over me like the incoming tide. They swirled like a whirlpool bringing images of Simone and the cold, lifeless body of Clifton, my son. My son.

I knew I'd never be able to sleep. I had to walk. Clear the cobwebs of painful memories from my mind. I grabbed my jacket I'd thrown on the only chair in the room and put it on. Stuffing the keys in my pocket, I headed down the stairs and back into the cold.

It was getting dark, but I didn't care. The shells made little snapping sounds as I stepped on them, working my way down the path behind the house. I knew I was getting closer to the ocean when I heard the rhythmic sound of the waves crashing over the sand. A strong smell of salt was in the air and the breeze had come up, bringing a chill to the air. The path opened up on a deserted beach. I could just make out the surf tickling the shore and clumps of seaweed scattered here and there. Careful where I put my feet, I made my way down the beach.

I was deep in thought when I heard a shout from behind me. Turning, I saw the beam from a flashlight bobbing its way toward me. I stopped and waited for whoever headed this way. Before she drew abreast of me, I could smell her perfume. In the glow from her flashlight, I saw it was Joanie.

"I saw you leave. Thought you might need a light to find your way back. Can't have my guests getting lost."

"Thanks. Must've gone farther than I thought," I said, glancing behind me.

"You're welcome. Come on, how about a hot cup of cocoa?" She beckoned with the light.

"Sounds great."

We walked in companionable silence, the gentle slap of the waves the only sound. Joanie shone the light when we reached the path, pale shells crunching beneath our feet. The rush of warm air that enveloped us when we let ourselves in felt good.

"Here we are. Safe and sound." Joanie shut off the flashlight and put it on a small table by the door. "Go ahead and make yourself comfortable. I'll be right back with the chocolate." She waved toward a door on her right.

I watched her disappear through another doorway, feeling like a void had been created when she left. She was like a breath of fresh air. *Was it a sign? Could I ever dare to love again?* I hoped it was in the cards for me. Perhaps this was the start of a new chapter in my life.

Chapter Thirty-Three

O'Malley sat at his desk and sipped his drink. Old Jim sure tasted good. He swirled the amber liquid in his glass and looked at the two diamonds in his palm. *Who would have thought an old knotted handkerchief could have held such treasure?* He raised his glass in a toast, envisioning a nice vacation in the tropics. Sun-tanned beauties serving him cocktails under a thatched hut, waves lapping at his feet. He smiled. "Thanks, Dexter." He shot the liquor home.

About the Author

Writing since she was a child, C.E. Zaniboni took the plunge into the world of fiction. From singer, actress, waitress, bartender, to owner of a small machine embroidery business, Chris has drawn from her many livelihoods to craft a novel set in the fictitious town of Gammil's Point, Maine. As a singer, Chris had the opportunity to entertain many with the program she and her mother, the late Dorothy York, put together, entitled, *Music Through The Years*. An actress in Community Theater, she had parts in many plays and musicals, some of them original works by local talent. While waitressing and bartending, Chris kept her ears open for material she knew she'd use in her writing. She lives with her husband in Mansfield, Massachusetts.

WEBSITE: czaniboni.com
FACEBOOK: https://www.facebook.com/icedat-midnight
OTHER: https://www.facebook.com/czaniboni

CPSIA information can be obtained
at www.ICGtesting.com
Printed in the USA
FSOW01n0323101117
40799FS